****

The Round Table

He just stood there a couple of feet from the counter looking down at his shoes not saying anything to anyone. He was ragged, warn and hollow eyed. People were moving around him putting in their orders.

I was sitting at the Round Table at the far end of the room. I was taking in what was happening at the end of the counter. No one was paying this guy the least bit of attention. I knew that he didn't have any money. He just stood there looking so lost. I got up and walked over to him at the counter.

"Hey fella, would you like a cup of coffee?" I asked him.

He raised his head, looked at me and nodded his head. I bought him a cup of coffee. He used a lot of creamer and a lot of sugar. He never said thank you or anything else. He just stirred his coffee and grabbed it with both hands and headed out of The Club. That was the first time I met Patrick.

Sitting at The Round Table and having given Patrick his morning coffee, my mind traveled back in time over twenty-five years. In fact, back to the time that a man came to The Round Table, the table was in a different building on a different street, but the table is the same. That man was shaking, very sick and in need of help. I remember that time as if it was yesterday. I truly can because

I was that man. Oh yeah, if only that round table could talk, the stories that it could tell could write a book.

I have always been an early riser and so I accepted the job of opening up the Club in the mornings to be available. I make four pots of coffee and make sure that the heat is on in the building when it's cold outside. I make sure the AA room is ready for the morning meeting. It is all volunteer work. I don't make a dime out of what I do, but what I get back is priceless; my sobriety.

I get here around 5 am to start getting things ready for the day ahead. Two or three street people will try and get a free cup of coffee out of me. I usually give it to them. We get all kinds that come through the doors down at The Club. I have heard many a story in the early morning hours. Some were heartbreaking, some were unbelievable and some were just plain old bullshit. Yeah, like I said, we get all kinds in the early morning hours at The Club.

The Round Table is filling up. My best friend Fred came in next. I always try to serve him when he gets there. Now, Fred is my senior by 14 years. I have known Fred for 15 years ever since he started hanging out at The Club. He is 82 years old. He comes in 2 to 3 times a week. He drives down from Arcata that's 8 miles north of Eureka. He usually gets to The Club around 7 am and then he and I will bullshit about anything under the sun. I guess that I should not say bullshit because some of the things we talk about are dead serious. But this morning, things seem to be on the lite side and not so serious.

The Club's History

Now the Club is not AA, but 99.99% of the people who go there are alcoholics. I am not pushing AA on you or anyone. I'm just telling you about a few that I have met. So if you're a "Normy", that's what we call people that can drink properly, don't worry you won't catch the disease from us. We in AA cannot call anyone an alcoholic. It's up to the individual themselves to say that they are one.

Now let me say this, I'm an alcoholic. I've been down many a hard road. Thanks to God and AA, I haven't had a drink in 35 years. I'm not bragging. I know that one little drink can take it away in the blink of an eye. I try to be a grateful man knowing that, "But for the grace of God, go

I." I just try to pass on what had been so freely given to me.

So right about now you might be thinking, "who is this telling me all this stuff?" Well, my name is John Stone. I'm a retired construction laborer and Timber Faller. I had a heart attack and stroke and was forced to quit working. Years of hard drinking to the point that almost killed me and finally brought me through the doors of AA. I got sober and have stayed that way for 35 years. I try to help those that want to get help for their drinkin' problem. I try to pay back for the kindness and caring that was given to me. I am what is known in AA as "A Trusted Servant."

OK, I've said enough about me. Let me tell you about a guy I shall call "Unlucky Joe". Joe has been coming around for a little over a year now. He has had go "back out" three or four times and test the waters. In the Big Book of AA, we call it research. Joe is in his early 30's. Hell of a nice young man when, he's not drinkin'.

"Well, John," Unlucky Joe said. "They got me again. God damn it! I'm the most unlucky person on this earth! This last Friday after I got off work, I thought I'd drop in at Ernie's place for just one or two beers before I went home. I thought to myself, "Hell a couple of beers ain't gonna hurt nothing!"

"I get to Ernie's," Joe says, "and one of my drinkin' buddies just happened to drop in. On my way home at 1:30 am, a red light shows up in my rear-view mirror! Dam it John, they got it in for me!"

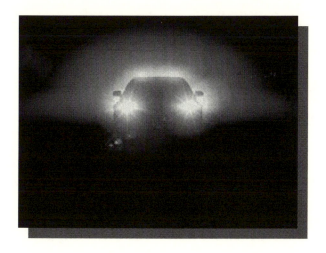

I laughed and asked, "They haul you in?"

"Yeah", he replied. "I'm going to have to pay a big ass fine!"

"Dam the luck," I said. "Don't you think Joe, that luck didn't have anything to do with this?" I asked him. "If you had not stopped at Ernie's and drank those beers, you would not have been hauled in for drunk driving! What do you think?"

"Yeah, I guess you're right," Joe said.

"Dam it anyway. I hope Joe, you realize that you cannot drink successfully. Not even a little bit. So Joe, it's up to you to realize if you are one of us or not. I'll say no more about it. I hope you keep coming back."

Ft. Bragg Trip

The days seemed to roll along, but the same old stuff was happening. I guess I was taking things for granted and feeling bored with my life. I know when I start getting like that I need to do something to get myself out of the funk. I decided I would spend a couple of days in Fort Bragg. I have family there; a son and a couple of brothers.

Well, I gave them the word down at The Club that I would see them later. I loaded up a card board box with a couple of T-shirts, shorts, pants and socks. I was only planning on staying a day or two. I gassed up my little Ford Focus and took off from Eureka about 9:30 am on a Wednesday or I think it was a Wednesday. Hell, every day is the same to me since I don't work anymore.

It was a nice clear morning. The rainy season was over and it was warming up. Just getting on the road seemed to make me feel better. I had my radio on listening to country music and sipping coffee. My driver's side window was down and the wind felt good coming in the car.

I was heading south on the 101 when my bladder told me I needed to find a place to relieve myself. I notice that I was coming to Pepperwood; not a town, just a spot on the road. I pulled off the 101 onto The Avenue of The Giants that used to be the old Highway 101. I went down into the giant redwood trees and found a place to pull off and park.

I hurried out of the car and walked back into the brush and started taking care of business. I zipped up my fly and headed back to the car. I heard a screech of tires up above me. A car stopped and then something came flying through the brush down the hill. The car pulled away quickly. I couldn't see what kind of car it was because of all the brush, but they were in a hurry to get gone!

I moved up the hill to see what was thrown through the brush. It was a back pack. I grabbed a hold of it and it was heavy. I started to unzip it and said to myself, "holly shit!" The back pack was stuffed full of bills with rubber bands wrapped around them! I zipped it back up. My heart was racing a hundred miles an hour! Dam! What do I do? What the hell should I do! Well hell, I'm not going to leave it here! So I grabbed it up and started down the hill to my car.

When I got back to my car, I started shaking all over. I tried to calm myself down. I unlocked my trunk and threw the back pack in and slammed it shut! Then I got in the car and just sat there thinking about what I was going to do next. I figured I had to get the hell out from where I was. I started my little car and headed back towards Eureka.

I changed my mind about going to Fort Bragg. I just wanted to get back to my apartment. I was starting to get a little paranoid. I felt like a thief or a or somebody bad. I would catch myself speeding then hit the brakes to slow down to the speed limit.

I kept checking my rear-view mirror to see if anyone was behind me. I finally made it home and pulled into my parking spot. I left the back pack in the trunk and hurried up to my upstairs apartment. I just wanted to get into my place and figure out what I was going to do with what I had in my trunk.

I told myself I was going to take a few days to figure this out. I knew that I could not tell anyone about this. I decided to keep the money. I asked myself why I felt like a thief or a bad person. Hell, I didn't steal it! I found it! Why was I feeling guilty?

That thought made me feel better. At least I wanted to think so. I would catch myself checking the traffic outside looking for big dark cars. By now, I'm sure that they would have come back to the place they had tossed the back pack down the hill and could not find it. I knew that there were some pissed off people, crazy people wanting their money back. They couldn't see my little red car through the brush could they? Did they see me? Those were the thoughts running through my head.

"Whoa John," I said to myself. "Slow down and calm down."

I turned on the TV and the news was on. They were talking about a shooting in some city back east. That was not what I needed to calm down. I turned the dam thing off! I went into the kitchen and fixed me a couple of sandwiches along with a glass of milk and got busy eating and thinking.

I did alright eating, but the bad part was my thinking. I kept getting all mixed up on it. I told myself that I didn't have to decide anything right away. I was going to sleep on it and that was that.

The next morning, I woke up early and decided to go down to The Club. I didn't go as early as I usually do. I wanted to give the person making coffee in my absence time enough to get things going. About 7 am, I headed out. When I walked into The Club, I saw Sam behind the counter.

"I thought you were going to Fort Bragg," Sam said to me.

I got my coffee and went over to The Round Table. My friends started coming in and it seemed like I was not my usual self. Earl and Fred were at the round table drinking coffee.

"What the hell is going on with you, John," Earl asked me. "You look like you are ready to jump out of your skin!"

"You said you were going to visit your family in Fort Bragg," said Fred.

I started to get defensive and said, "Can't a man change his mind around here! What are you guys trying to do? Get rid of me!"

Well, things finally calmed down inside of me enough that I could finally get to talk about something or somebody else. Another morning passed at The Club. After I returned to my apartment, I unlocked the trunk of my car and grabbed the back pack and hauled it upstairs to my apartment. I went into my bedroom and tossed it into my closet. I knew right then and there what I was going to do with the money. I am just not that type of guy that could leave something like this just hanging without dealing with it.

John Becomes Robin Hood

While sitting at my kitchen table, I came to this conclusion, "I am not giving this money to the police."

But I also knew that I wouldn't feel right keeping the money for myself. I was going to give it away! With that thought in my mind, I started to feel better. The how's, why's and who's to give the money to I could figure out as I went along. Since I found the money in The Avenue of The Redwoods and I was going to give the money to the needy, I decided to call myself Robin Hood of The Redwoods!

Yeah by God, I was feeling better! I had better open up that back pack and count how much money was in it! I went to my bedroom, grabbed the backpack, unzipped it and dumped it onto my bed. Wow! What a site! Hundred-dollar bills with rubber bands around them scattered all over my bed. It really was hell keeping all this to myself and not telling anyone else.

Bam's Life Story

My birth certificate says, Mathew Dillon Davis, but I go by Bam. I was born in some little town in Oklahoma. Don't know the name of it and don't give a dam if I find out its name.

My mother got tired of my old man getting drunk and beating the shit out of her. So on one Sunday morning she just went out the door and never came back. That just left me and that mean son of a bitch. I was supposed to call my dad. He started taking things out on me and there was nothing I could do about it until, I was 15 years old. He would get drunk, yell and kick me and take his frustrations out on me. The last night I spent under his roof, I found me a lead pipe about two feet long and an inch and a half in diameter. I kept it in my bedroom closet.

Then, it happened. He was out late and came in drunk yelling at me cussing and kicking me. I got away from him, went to my closet and got the pipe.

I came back and swung it and hit him in one of his lower legs. I stood there over him as he looked up at me in fear.

"I should kill you, you rotten son of a bitch!" I yelled at him.

I left that night and that was the last I've seen of that the man who was my father. I hitch hiked up to my cousins who lived two towns away and stayed for two days. Then, I started thumbing it for the west coast and ended up in L.A. Sleeping on the streets, getting enough to eat was a full-time job at first. I had to learn fast and I did. I got to be tough and fast. I had to run and I ran a lot.

After I had been in East L.A. for about a week, I came across this man called Graso. I don't know why he was called Graso, but that is the name he went by. He was sitting on a bench and I knew he was watching me, so I went up to him for some change for my next meal. He was about 30 to 40 years old.

He laughed and said, "You new in this town, boy? You look like you could use a little help. You gonna find that you don't get something for nothing in this town. So sit down and let's talk for a little while, OK?"

I was hungry with no place to go, so I sat down on the bench next to him and he started telling me how it was about the street life in L.A. and if, you want to make it here you had to get a job.

"I can get you a job," he told me. "You may not want it, but I'll run it by you, OK? I already have a couple of young lads working for me."

That is when I was told about shop lifting and how to pull it off without getting caught or so I was told. I was so desperate that I took him up on it. That started my life of crime. I went to reform schools and in and out of jails. I did learn how to make it out there. I learned to trust nobody and to use fear for my benefit. Whatever I tried to do, I tried to be the best. It was usually against the law. I learned to pick locks, steal cars and how to bypass alarms systems for breaking and entering. If there were things, I could take what people were keeping inside would bring me some money, I'd steal it!

All this brought me to the escapade that I am in now. Like I've said before, I like the east side of L.A. It's where I first landed and where I always went back to. I was sleeping in an abandoned building on Kenard street. It was right across from the salvage yard where they crushed autos and piled up scrap metal on what looked like a 10-acre lot. They had a crane with an electric magnet separating the piles. They kept their crushers off to one side. I got me this job at a car wash, about 1/2 mile away until, I could figure out what I was going to do next. I don't like paying rent and I don't if I can find a way not to.

I came across this abandoned building on Kenard street one evening, I seen there was a busted door at the rear. I went in and checked it out. There was dust and dirt all over the place. I seen what looked like a rickety stair case that led up to a loft. I carefully went up them and found that there was floor space enough to put down my sleeping bag. It was good enough for me to spend my nights there. I got cut loose from Ironwood

State prison two months ago and was starting over one more time the story of my life.

As I laid down in my sleeping bag waiting for sleep to overtake me, my mind took me back to when, I first arrived here in L.A. I was a 15-year-old kid scared to death with nothing or no one to get help from. It wasn't long before I got sent to Ventura Youth Correctional Facility. There, I learned to fight, to watch, to see and to remember what skills I use now. I became a loner. I didn't get a buddy or hang with anyone. I tried to mind my own business and keep out of other people's lives, but there will always be in life the ones there to test you. I'm glad that I'm tough. I must have gotten it from my Mom cause I know I didn't get it from my chicken ass old man.

Right soon after being there, about four of them surrounded me and their leader's name was Lenny.

"Hey new boy," said Lenny. "This is your day of finding out how things are done in here and I am your teacher," he laughed. "What I say, goes and your first job is to do what I say. You understand?"

Then, he laughed again. He came up to me nose to nose. That was too much and was too close. I hit the son of a bitch with everything I had and he went down in a flash. I had moved onto the next closest guy. One punch to the solar plexus and he hit the dirt too. The other two took off.

That is where I got the name "Bam". The word got around that you didn't mess with the new guy or else "Bam", you went down for the count. The name stuck and I was alright with it. They left me alone. A few tried to get friendly, but I didn't go for that. I spent my time alone waiting and watching and learning. But most of all, I remembered what I had learned.

After about a week of sleeping in this old shell of a building, I started to take in the more and more of my surroundings. As I've said before on the other side of the street was a salvage and wrecking yard. It had a sign that said "Spartan Salvage and Wrecking Yard".

You could barely read it, it was so faded and worn. There was a small window that over looked the street facing the office of the salvage yard.

It was grimy with dirt, so dirty you could barely see out of it. It had six different panes. One of the panes was busted with about a three-inch hole in one of the panes.

Before settling down one evening, I walked over to the window and looked out. I could see across the street and see the right side of the salvage office. There was a window upstairs and I could see inside. They had blinds, but they were open. I have always been observant of what is going on around me.

One day I looked in at this upstairs window and took in what was in that room as much as I could see. What caught my eye right off was this desk and on the wall behind was a picture I saw that looked like John D. Rockefeller.

The picture seemed to be about three feet tall and a couple of feet wide from this distance. I couldn't be sure, but that's who it looked like to me. I heard about John D. Rockefeller while I was doing time at Iron Wood. I read a book in there about John D. and they had a picture of an old man on the cover that looked like the picture hanging on the wall.

So, I started looking out my window into the window across the street. I had finished my day at the car wash and came back early to my loft. I went over to my window and looked out. The blinds were open in the building across the street on the upper floor.

There was a man sitting at the desk. He was talking on a land line phone. He seemed to be shouting. After a bit, he slammed the phone down. He wrote something down on a piece of paper, stood up and turned around, went to the picture on the wall and then, me watching paid off! He went to the picture, put his hand on the left corner of the picture and it swung out to the right and there it was, a safe. He dialed in his

numbers, opened up the safe and put the paper inside. He moved to his left a little and I could tell there was an alarm system. He lifted the cover, punched in a few numbers, closed the safe and swung the picture of John D. to cover the safe and then, went out of my sight.

I was proven right. A minute later he came out the front door of the building and got into what looked like a Ford Bronco and drove off. I started putting together all that I saw across the street and what I was going to do next. One thing I learned in life, there was always a "next". The following day, I went to my car wash job. I quit and went and bought me a telescope. I didn't buy and expensive one. I just needed to see real good across the street. I brought it into my loft and set it up on a tripod. I started dialing it in on the upstairs window across the street. I had this feeling inside me about this outfit across from me. I didn't know what it was, but I had it, so I started watching across the street. The guy I started calling "Bronco Man" would show up around 10 am.

He was no early riser. He would stay until about noon, then he would leave. Sometimes, he would come back around 4:30 or 5 pm. At other times, he never came back. I took it he didn't work on a regular time line. I have learned how to wait and not be impatient. I learned that in prison life. So, I made up my mind to watch and wait and see what happens.

I could see real good after dialing in my telescope. I was right about the picture covering the safe. It was John D. Rockefeller. That gave me a laugh. I took it he wasn't worried about people looking in on him through the side window from an old abandoned building across the street. Or, I guess he thought, who knows?

But my luck held anyway, he didn't close the blinds and I could see in. He did not go into his safe the rest of the week, but on the wall to the left at the very edge of my sight was his security system. It was a Moose 2100 with a key and key pad entry. I had seen them before in my line of work. You raised the lid from the bottom and punched in some numbers on the key pad to disarm the alarm. It was like looking over his right shoulder at the key pad.

It took me three times to confirm the numbers, but by the third time, I had it down. I had me a note pad and I wrote the numbers in it.

Now for the safe, when was the son of a bitch going to open it up! I had to wait for three more days. I was watching Bronco Man and again, he was on the phone. It was like the last time. He seemed to be yelling, hung up the phone, wrote something on a piece of paper, stood up, turnaround and went to our boy, J.D. Rockefeller! He put his hand on the bottom left, where there was a way to unlock the picture all the way back and I got a complete view of the safe! I had my telescope dialed in and I brought it in as if I was standing right there in front of the dam safe.

My heart gave a leap at first, but I calmed myself down and got down to business. Here we go! He spun the dial to the right and then, he slowed down and stopped at 29. Then, back to the left one complete run and came to a stop at 17. He turned it to the right and stopped at good old 50! He grabbed the handle and opened the safe and put the paper in. I could not see clearly into the safe and he had only opened it for only a second! I got what I watched for and waited for my next move.

I saw that they had a real genuine junk yard dog. The dog looked like he had a lot of Pit Bull and who knows what else. They left him in the yard, behind the metal fence that surrounded the place. I could hear him bark and gnarl at people, if they happened to walk by at night, He was a mean looking son of a bitch all right. I was going to have to get into the office and into that safe!

The routine that I had, before I quit my job at the car wash, was walk over to Wally Stubben's house once or twice a week to take a shower and change clothes.

I met Wally, about was10 years back and how that came about is, I was walking on, can't remember what street, but two dudes were harassing this old man as I walked on the scene. Two young guys bullying this old man pissed me off and turned me mean!

"What the fuck are you two doing!" I yelled at them.

"None of your dam business," one of them answered.

"Well, I'm making it my business as of now!" I told them as I approached.

Before he came back with an answer, I hit the bastard right between the eyes and down he went. I grabbed the other by the throat and kicked him in the balls. It was all over very shortly.

"Are you OK old man?" I asked Wally.

"Yeah, fella you saved my ass," Wally replied. "I live just a short ways from here. Do you want to come over to my place? I need to get home!"

We left the two scumbags there and I followed Wally home. That is when our friendship began, if you care to call it friendship. Wally didn't ask a lot of questions and I got right to the point. I told him I was looking for a place to shower and change clothes. I let him know that I didn't want to live there, but come and go as I please. He listened.

"I think that we can make a deal," Wally said. "If you could bring me old Jim Beam over once and a while, we just might come to an agreement."

Like I said, that was over 10 years ago. Wally has a girlfriend a few miles away and when they are getting along, Wally will stay at her place. When not, he's back at his place. Right now, they must be getting along, he has only been around to check his mail and check on things.

Wally has a carport on the side of his house. I talked him into letting me park my ride in it. Wally doesn't drive and, like I said, as long as Jim Beam shows up every so often, he was happy. I walked or rode the buses and only used my car for travels or for my jobs.

I had made up my mind that I was going to follow up and break into Bronco Man's safe. First things first; the dog. Second, getting into the office and third, getting into the safe! Once that is done, I'll need to get the hell out of town for a good long while. I don't know how much money is in the safe or if any at all! Hopefully, there will be enough for the trouble of getting into it. Some kids grow up to be doctors and lawyers. I grew up breaking into people's houses and businesses or maybe, I just haven't grown up, yet. It's what I've done my whole life. I don't apologize for it, it's just what I do.

This evening, while lying in my sleeping bag, I was turning things over in my head. I needed to get things in order, so I can get on with what I have to do to pull this next job off.

The dog, the dam dog that is hanging out in the salvage yard, that was on the top of my list.

While doing time in Ironwood, this last time, there was this guy named, Steny.

He was a pharmacist or used to be. He got rolled up for selling some pills illegally. His ass wound up in Ironwood! I helped him out over a couple of things, so he owed me a few favors. He gave me his mother's and father's phone number and said if I wanted to get in touch with him, to call the number he wrote down. Don't know why I hung onto that little piece of paper, but I did.

The next morning, I called that number and got his mother on the phone and told her I was one of Steny's friends and that I want to look him up. I told her him and I met in Ironwood and became friends and that I was going straight and hope he was too. She was a little leery, but then she gave me his phone number and told me to tell him to call his mother. I told her that I would.

I called him and damned if he didn't answer! It surprised the hell out of him, but I told him I had a dog next door that I wanted to put out of commission for a few hours and needed something to take care of that.

Steny didn't miss a beat. He never got nosy or asked a lot of questions.

"Bam, I owe you one and I got what you need and it will do the job," said Steny. "Bring yourself over here to my place and we'll get you taken care of, OK? Better yet, why don't we meet at Taco Bell."

I had told him where I was, but off by a couple of blocks. I did not want anyone knowing where I was staying. So, me and Steny met at Taco Bell and ordered a few tacos and he handed over a container of pills.

"Bam, these are Special K, Ketamine pills," said Steny. "They will do the job that you want done. I gave you a dozen pills and two hours later, that dog won't be barking, walking or doing anything, but snoozing. So, good luck to you, Bam. Take care, no charge, OK?"

We shook hands and I left him and headed back to my place. Now, to get things ready for when I make my move. I need to make sure my wheels is gassed up, check the oil and tires. I decided that I was going to head north for a few days, until things cooled down. I decided on doing my job on Friday night, when everyone was starting their weekend. That would be six days. So, I need to start getting things ready for Friday.

Two days later at about 3 pm in the afternoon, a big black limo pulls up to the salvage yard and three men get out and start heading into the office. One man of about 60 years old and who you could tell was in charge with a much younger man close beside him who looked like a "Yes" man and was there to do the older man's bidding.

Then, there was the driver. He was big and all muscle and about 30-40 years old. The driver unlocks the trunk and takes out two suitcases and falls in behind the other two as they head into the office. I have been around this world long enough to know that this was not a, "thought I'd drop by and see how you're doing" visit. No, something was up. They went into the building. I watched and a little bit later, the blinds were closed on the window facing the street. I smiled and said to myself, "sorry people, you're a little late for that." They were there for only a short time. They left, minus the two suit cases. Things were getting more interesting with each passing day.

Friday finally arrives and my car is all gassed up and in good running order. Everything I have inside this old building moved out and in my car.

I went to the butcher shop, got a big old steak and my lock picking tools handy. Now, I wait for the sun to go down and start to go down and start getting dark. "Did I forget anything", I asked myself. Well, if I did it is too late now!

5 O'clock and the workers are pulling out of the salvage yard. Bronco Man left the office right at 5 pm. I cut slits in the steak and shoved the Ketamine pills in between them. I used all the pills and hope that will do.

At 10:30 pm, I leave the loft, go down stairs, go out the broken back door and head across the street to the fence in front of the salvage yard. Sure enough, here come that big mean son of a bitch. He came growling and slamming up against fence trying to get at me! I unwrapped the steak and tossed it over the fence. The situation got different real fast. He grabbed that steak and headed back behind the office. I stood by the fence for another minute. It got real quiet. That made me feel a little better. Now back to my place to wait for a couple hours.

12 O'clock midnight, down the stairs and across the street I went. All is quiet. I'm at the gate. I get out my lock picking tools and I soon have the gate lock opened. I go in and put the gate back into place, so as not to look suspicious.

Now the front door, a simple lock system and inside I am! I have with me a back pack and an extra cloth bag to put stuff in. I turn on my pen light and now, I see a beat-up old desk with file and papers scattered all over it. If I was guessing, I'd say it was the time keeper's desk.

The stairwell was to the right side of the room and up the stairs I go and I'm at the last door

I have to get through. My lock picking tools do the job, again. I was in Bronco Man's office! Now, it's over to the alarm system. I get my numbers out of my pocket, open the alarm and punch in my numbers. One has only a minute or so to do this or the alarm goes off. Done! I tell myself to slow down, calm down, but stay alert and be ready for almost anything.

Next, the wall behind the desk and to old John D. Rockefeller I went! I put my hand to the bottom left and felt a button. I pushed it and John D. swung out to the right. I remembered the numbers to the safe. Here we go! I spin the dials to the right and stopped at 29. Then, to the left one complete turn, stopped at 17.

Then back to the right and stopped at 50. OK now, we'll see if all this waiting and watching is going to pay off.

I turn the handle and pull open the door to the safe. I shine my pen light inside and my heart almost stopped. I could not believe my eyes. The safe was packed with money!

I mean packed! I turned off the pen light. Then, turned it back on again to make sure that I wasn't dreaming!

OK, now let's get down to business. I started filling the backpack. When it got filled, I stuffed the rest into the cloth sack that I brought along. I was wearing gloves just in case they checked for prints. I closed the safe and thanked old John D. I reset the alarm system and locked the door too.

I went out the front to the gate and locked it and went out on the street. I was moving fast to one block over, where my car was parked.

I was almost to my car when, head lights hit me from behind. My heart dropped. I kept walking. The car passed me and kept going. I could finally breathe, again.

Reaching the car, I opened the trunk and then threw the cloth sack in. I took off the back pack and tossed it in too. My heart was racing even though I kept telling myself that I was almost there. "Now get yourself behind the wheel and get started out of town"! I yelled to myself.

BAM off to Oregon with a Backpack and Sack of Cash!

After driving all night my nerves were on a razor's edge. Driving up the 101 highway and heading to Oregon, I knew I was going to have to stop some place and rest up in order to continue.

Crazy! Dam, everything was just crazy as hell. It was as if I was in a dream world and none of this was real. But it's alright and I'm running for my life. I have a backpack full of money I heisted, yesterday. I keep seeing this car I think that has been following me all night. I don't see it now, but I'm about to jump out of my skin! Dam! I got to get some rest or I'm going to lose it all.

Rolling and heading north on I-5, I turned on the radio and then, after a minute or so, I turned it back off. I can't seem to get my insides to calm down. Got to get miles between me and LA. Why am I so god damn nervous and jumpy as hell? That's usually not me. Is it because of the big haul that I made which I can still hardly believe is real? Whatever it is, I need things to get back to normal for me.

Then, I feel the steering wheel starting to pull to the left. Dam, what is it?

Better pull off and check it out. I see a sign and it said, Valencia 5 "Miles Ahead" and one for a

Texaco gas station too. When I got to the exit and pull off, I see smoke coming out of the front left wheel, dam! I don't need this! Just when I was starting to calm down, I pull off the road to the gas station and see smoke coming off the front left wheel.

Then, walks in the man behind the counter and says, "I seen you pull in, looks like you have a wheel problem. Can I help you?"

"I sure hope so," I replied. "I think I'm going to need a tow truck and get a shop to fix my left front wheel."

"I can do that," he told me.

He got on the phone and in a minute or so later he let me know that his friend Jack would be here to fix the problem and offered me a cup of coffee.

"No thanks," I replied. "I'll just wait for him at my car."

Cars were coming in, gassing up, then moving on. They seem to be quite busy. Looking around and seen that no one was paying any attention. I opened the trunk and grabbed the cloth bag, put my hand inside and pulled out two rolls of bills and put them inside my coat pocket. I then closed the trunk and opened up the driver's side door, got in and waited.

What seemed to be about 45 minutes then, the tow truck showed up. I told him that I needed the nearest repair shop, paid him and he hooked up my car, got it all ready to tow, then told me to hop in the passenger side of his truck and we headed out.

He was a hell of a chatty bastard. He asked me all kinds of questions; where I was going and what did I do for a living. I told him one lie after another. Some people are like plain nosy and this guy was one of them. I kept my answers short. I think he finally figured out that I didn't want to talk and finely shut up. We soon arrived at Steve's Auto Repair Shop. I went into the shop, while ole chatty was unhooking. I hollered out "hello" and a guy in coveralls came out from under a Chevy van.

"Can I help you?" he asked me.

About that time, Old Chatty came in and said, "Hi Steve, I brought you some business. I got a call for another tow or so, I got to get going. Be seeing you later."

Steve grabbed a rag from his hip pocket and wiped his hands. We shook hands and he told me that he would take a look and see what the problem is. He took the floor jack out to my car and jacked the front left front wheel. He soon had the wheel off.

"Well sir, looks like you've fried your left front wheel," he told me. "You are going to need to replace the whole wheel assembly. That spindle is fried."

I told him to do whatever it took to get my car on the road. We went back in the shop and he got on the phone. He then, after a bit, hung up telling me that he can have the parts here tomorrow and with luck of having no problems, have me back on the road in a couple days.

"OK," I said. "Do what you have to do. I'll call you tomorrow and see how things are going. So, if you'll call me a cab, I'll let you get on with things."

Sitting on the bed in the Sundowner motel in room #8 I was doing what I've done all my life and that is, wait. I tell myself that I cannot change the way things are so, try and unwind and think about what you have to do next. Why am I heading for Oregon? I remember back when I was around 10 years old my Mom would tell me stories of when she was a young girl about all the good times she had. She said that Oregon was good. Her eyes would light up when she talked about those times.

So, Oregon is a good enough place to make a new start. if I keep a low profile and keep things small and don't go crazy on spending this money that I got.

Dam, I can hardly believe that there is a back pack with all this money and a sack with more money in it waiting to be taken to Oregon. But I need to remember to stay on guard. There are some mad sons of bitches looking for their money in L.A.

After putting the back pack and money sack in the closet, shaving, taking a hot shower and changing clothes, I wanted to be ready so if someone comes in through that hotel door. So, I'll sleep in my clothes and be on my guard until, I get the hell out of California! I know that this is a hell of a way to live, but that is the way that it is. Maybe, when I get to Oregon things will change.

Laying back on the bed my mind went back to those early years in life. The only time that I could ever remember being the least bit happy in my life was when my mother taught me how to lose myself in books. The library became my place to go to get outside of myself; peace of mind. From that time on, I became an avid reader and that time included behind bars.

Some may think that I would have turned against my mother for leaving that Sunday after taking all that abuse that she had been taking day after day, but I did not. All I wanted was for her to find a safe place to be around people that treated her good. My mind was racing around as I lay in bed for a long time finally, falling into a stressful sleep.

Steve finally got the car fixed after staying in the motel two nights. I was ready to be on the road again. Gassed up, paid Steve the mechanic and I was now moving North! After putting L.A. further behind with each passing mile feeling better inside. Deciding on taking the coastal route moving over to highway 101 by taking a left at Williams on highway 20 going through Clear Lake and coming out at Capella then, shooting North for Oregon. I began to have that feeling of maybe, just maybe I am going to get to make a new start.

Bam Meets Bronco Man

The air seems to be fresher. I felt like I did when, I was leaving prison. I was now in the mountains amongst the giant redwoods of northern California. I had been pushing it since I left L.A. I was tired. I was going to have to rest up soon.

Just south of Pepperwood Rd., I noticed a car that looked just like Bronco Man's Bronco following me. Whoever it was, was driving like a bat out hell and slammed right into my back bumper. What the hell! How in the hell did he find me! I saw Bronco Man get out of the car with a baseball bat in his hand running at my car! I hit the gas pedal and got the hell out of there.

The only thing I could think about was that bag of cash. I was driving recklessly, but had no other choice. I didn't want them to catch me with all that money. After screeching around a few more corners, I saw a place on the right and pulled over and released the trunk hatch. I got out and grabbed the backpack and slung it down the hill into the bushes. I jumped back in the car, slammed the pedal to the metal and got the hell out of there.

I made sure to remember the spot. These bastards are going to catch me, so I better go out fighting. At the next wide spot, I wheeled the car over and started looking for a weapon.

Sure enough, that Bronco came around the corner and pulled over right in front of me. The driver slammed his hand down on the left side and grabbed his baseball bat! He leaped out of the Bronco and headed for my car.

I knew dam good and well that it was the man that I had robbed. I remembered that I had stashed an old .38 Colt revolver I bought back from the pawn shop to keep myself safe with the money. I reached into my glove box and pulled out the .38 and started getting out of my car. Before, I could get out all the way, Bronco Man clocked me in the side of the head and knocked me down on the ground.

I looked up and he was going to hit me again. I pointed the .38 at Bronco Man and shot him dead. It took me a while to be able to stand up after being clocked by the bat. I shook it off and realized that I needed to clean up after this mess. I decided to put Bronco Man's body in the trunk of my car. So, I grabbed the keys of the Bronco out of his pocket.

I drug Bronco man's body to the back of my car and lifted his body into the trunk and slammed the lid shut. I took the sack of cash that I did not throw down the hill out of my car and put it in the Bronco. I went back to my car, got in and put it in neutral and turned the steering wheel straight towards the cliff.

I got out and pushed my car and it slowly rolled off the cliff. I looked down to make sure that it could not be seen from above and lucked out that it had rolled into a bunch of sage bushes and well hid.

I had a huge relief! Bronco man was just like me, a thief. It was him or me and that is the way it is in the business he learned early in life in the pen. I got into the Bronco and headed back up the road to get his back pack full of the money I stole from the man I just shot and killed!

Arriving back at the spot he threw the back pack, he parked, got out and looked down the hill.

It was filled with brush, so he couldn't see it. He started down the hill taking his time and checking the place out fully; he came up empty handed.

"Dam!" Bam yelled. "I was gone here from here for just a few minutes. Where the hell is my backpack!"

Walking on down the lower road, he saw an RV parked and a man sitting outside of it in a lawn chair drinking coffee. Bam went to him and asked him if he saw anyone loading up a back pack.

"Funny you should ask that," the man in the lawn chair replied. "I've been parked here for a while. A little red Ford Focus, around 2002 or 3, pulled in and was only here for a short time only. I saw the guy unlock his trunk and throw something in and then, take off heading north. The reason I noticed was because, I used to own a Ford Focus. I'm a guy that likes to see things that most people don't.

There was a string of flower petals hanging from his rear-view mirror and his license plate had a Warriors covering his plate. I hope that this helps you out. Would you like a cup of coffee?"

"No thank you," Bam said. "I gotta go!" I headed back up the hill to his car. All he could do now was drive like hell and hope that he could catch up to that little red Focus hoping he wasn't stopped by the CHP. It all came down to luck, now. Was the guy in the RV telling the truth?

Why in the hell did I throw that back pack down the hill anyway? I was afraid and panicked.

I'm not going to get that money back by crying about it. Like I said, 'It all comes down to luck.'

Passing everything on the road going north and no CHP and coming into the south end of Eureka, he spotted a red Focus. Pulling up behind it, he noticed the Warriors license plate cover and flower petals hanging from the rear-view mirror. He had found his man! Now, to just hang back and follow this man to where he goes.

Following him to an apartment complex on Fairfield St. He now knew where he lived or so he thought. He got out and walked back to where the car was telling himself to go slow and don't push things.

So, get yourself a room and get me some rest. You got to pull yourself together. So, get out of here and come back in the morning.

On the same street, just a few blocks down was the Bayview motel, that would do. Then, I would follow the man I was after and get my money back.

As I got ready for bed, I thought it a good idea to take a hot shower and clean up after getting hit in the head with a baseball bat from Bronco Man. I looked in the mirror and saw that I had a huge bulge in the right side of my head and was feeling a bit dizzy. I've had a few knocks to the head and decided to lay down before, I fell down.

I woke up the next morning not at The Bayview Motel, I woke up in the hospital. A nurse walked in and told me that I was found two weeks ago unconscious in his bed by the housekeeper. She let me know that my Bronco was safe at the motel and that all of my personal belongings were safely locked in the Bronco.

I got released from the hospital, got a cab and went over to the Bayview hotel. I was not sure if that money was in the Bronco and already had plans in my head on how to deal with it; bad thoughts. If that money is in there, I'm gonna pay them well. If my money is not in the Bronco, I'm gonna do the same to them as I did to Bronco Man!

I got to the motel and the owner was there and hands me the keys. They go out to the back and I open the door and there, low and behold in the back is my sack of cash that I did not throw with the back pack, thank God!

The owner smiles, "It's all in there, Bam."

I pull out $500 and gives it to the owner and hightailed it out of there to find the man in the Focus! He goes over to his place and I see no car. I waited for a bit and then, decided to go get myself a beer and shoot some pool hoping to get some info. from the locals.

I see Ernie's Bar and pull over. I haven't had a drink in years after realizing that I didn't want to be like my S.O.B. Dad that drove my mother out of my life. Alcoholism runs in the family.

The bar tender pours me a cold draft and lets me know that many people know the man that drives that Focus, but he hasn't been in here in over 30 years. He gave up drinking. They all let him know that the place to find him was at The Club. He goes over to the Club and they let him know that John, that was his name, is on a trip and not sure when he'd be back. I could tell that they were suspicious and did not want to tell me too much. I told them that I was helped by John and wanted to thank him personally. The only thing that I found out was his name; John.

I went on a bender at Ernie's. I eventually got kicked out and realized that if I kept it up, I would be arrested and they'd find out about the heist I pulled off! I better sober up and the best place to do that would be where he could find John, The Club.

I started to go to The Club and attend AA meetings and kept hearing of how much John has been helping out The Club for years. Told me that he has a friend that is going to buy them a new location for the Club.

It began to soak in that John was spending that money on helping others and had not bought himself a fancy car and house! This John fella must be doing God's work with that money that I stole and killed a man for! Things really started to sink in and I decided to get an AA Big Book and learn about this AA thing.

I got the book and read it. I listened to how others had been brought up like me and lead bad lives of robbing, stealing and cheating. I was a selfish little boy carrying around nothing but old bags of guilt and remorse from things I'd done to others and others had done to me.

I got a sponsor that knew John and worked the steps. People began to know me, but I kept that heist and John with my money to myself. I knew that I had to meet him and resolve this one way or another.

My sponsor told me that John was on his way back to Eureka and he was going to be one of the speakers tonight at the evening meeting. I did some praying asking for God to help me resolve this big issue. I was scared I was going to kill him.

Alcoholics
Anonymous
This is the Second Edition of
the Big Book, New and Revised.
The Basic Text for Alcoholics Anonymous.

Robin Hood's First Adventure: Sacramento

So after having made up my mind on what I was going to do or at least what I thought I was going to do. I got my little Focus loaded with what little I was going to take with me. So, no more "what ifs" running through my mind. I was ready to leave Eureka and start this new adventure that was about to start.

Heading south on the 101, I started to get a little bit giddy about what lay ahead of me. The people I was going to meet and the place's I was going to see. This ole retired logger has not been very many places and I felt like a little kid inside. There is a lot of that, that can be said about not knowing what lays ahead in one's life. *"Don't get carried away John and take this trip one day at a time,"* I said to myself.

Just south of Willits, I came to highway 20 going over to Lake County and taken onto I-5. It seemed like in no time, I was at I-5 and decided to go south. The next road sign I came to said, "Sacramento 58 Miles". It was at that time I decided that was a good place to start my great adventure.

After making it to Sacramento, I pulled off at the first exit and there was a Motel 6 with a little park next to it. I checked in, took a much-needed shower, grabbed a cup of coffee at the front desk and headed over to the park across the street to gather my thoughts.

While sitting on the bench in the city park, the sun was shining and it sure felt good on these old bones of mine. I closed my eyes and took in the sounds. There were swings making sounds like that of a gate as kids were swinging. Close by, a mother was yelling at her son.

"Bobby you be careful on those monkey bars," his mother yelled. "You hear me!"

It was summer in full swing! My mind drifted back to when I was a small boy playing in a park somewhat like this one that brought back a smile to my face. I had my head down and was feeling the warm sun on the back of my neck.

Then, I got this feeling that someone was watching me. I raised my head and opened my eyes. There standing directly in front of me was a little girl looking me in the eyes.

"Was you sleepin', mister?" she asked me.

"No, honey." I laughed. "I was just resting my eyes for a while. Us older people have to do that sometimes."

She just stood there looking at me. She had the widest and biggest grin I had seen in long time.

"What's your name sweetheart?" I asked her.

"My name is Alice and I'm four and half years old," she said.

"Well Alice, I was going to guess that," I said. "Thanks for letting me know that."

There she was, a freckled faced, sun bleached blonde little angel. She had a summer top on with a teddy bear on the front of it and a red little skirt. Her clothes were clean, but they were well worn. Most of all, I noticed her shoes. They looked like they were cheap plastic with cracks in them. I pointed at the bear on her summer top and asked her if he had a name.

"He sure does," she said. "His name is Billy Boy."

"How did he get his name," I asked her.

"It was his name when he was born," she said.

"Dog gone it, I should have known that," I said.

What the heck is wrong with me anyway? I think Billy Boy is a real good name for a bear. I seen a woman in her early twenties coming across the park.

"Alice, we have to go now," the lady told Alice.

"Oh mommy, I'm having so much fun here in the park," Alice replied. "Do we have to go now?"

"Yes, we have to go now," said her mother. "Maybe, we will come back tomorrow, OK?"

"OK, mommy," Alice said.

She grabbed her mother's hand and they walked to the other side of the park where their beat-up old Chevy was parked. They climbed in and then, I heard the starter grinding and after a while it started.

It smoked like hell and one could see that it was on its last legs or should I say, wheels. They drove off, smoke and all leaving me to myself and my thoughts.

I hope that Alice's mother didn't think that I was a sick old pervert, when it came to little kids. God knows this world has a lot of them. I know that would put a bad hurt on someone that tried to pull that kind of stuff on kids.

Thinking again of little Alice, I thought I would head back to my motel room, take a shower and get ready for an AA meeting. I got in my car and started off.

After driving a few blocks, I happened to see a toy store. Acting on an impulse, I found a parking place. I parked, got out and went into the toy store. There was toys of all kinds, but I was looking for one "Special Toy". A young lady came up to me.

"Can I help you," she said. "Are you looking for something?"

"I sure am," I said. "I'm looking for a Teddy bear about 3 feet tall. You got anything like that?"

"Follow me," she said.

I followed her and sure enough, there was a bunch of Teddy Bears of all different sizes. I spotted one. She handed it to me. It was about 3 feet tall. I paid for it, went out to the car and tossed the bear into the back seat and headed to the motel.

Early next morning sitting in the cafe that was close to the motel, I was having breakfast tossing down some ham and eggs with a cup of good old eye-opening coffee! I was doing some heavy thinking. I do some of my best thinking in the early mornings. So, what was my plans for this day? I planned on going back to that park hoping that "Little Alice" and her mother would show up there, so I could give Alice that big teddy bear I was hauling around in my back of my seat.

Now, I don't know about other people, when it comes to talking to one's self, but I do it all the time. I try not to do it out loud. It can draw a lot of funny looks from people, so I try to keep it inside most of the time. I made up my mind just to play it by ear. That is what I have been doing ever since I started this great adventure of mine. I just keep on doing it that way.

After having eaten and a few cups of coffee in me, I left the waitress a nice tip then, wandered back to my car. I found the address of the Alano Club in town where I could hang out for a while. I came in and a guy named Ralph was behind the counter.

He seen I was a visitor and not a local. He made me welcome to his town and his club.

He handed me a schedule of all the AA meetings and told me to keep coming back. Now to most people who have a problem with booze, it's like throwing out a welcome mat, so I hung out at the Alano, till about 2 o'clock. Then, I headed to the park.

I arrived and it was a beautiful day. The sun was warming things up. Some people was there already with kids along with their parents. I looked around to see if Alice and her mother was there, but I didn't see them.

So, I just sat on the same bench I sat on yesterday and proceeded to take it easy. There was a dad in the middle of the park with what looked like and 8 or 9-year-old boy trying to get a kite up into the air. There wasn't much wind blowing and they were having a hell of a time trying to get that kite airborne.

The boy looked like he could go all day, but the dad looked he was going to drop any minute. I just whiled away the day sitting *on that bench.*

Then I heard that same sound I heard yesterday of a starter grinding away. I looked up and sure enough it was Alice and her mother in that old beat up old Chevy trying to get it started. I don't know how I missed her, but I did. Well, she kept on grinding away to get that old clunker started.

Finally, there was just a click and nothing else. I got to my feet walked over to their car.

Alice's mother had her head down with her hands on the steering wheel and looked like she was crying. She had the driver's side window down.

She looked up as I approached the door. Yes, she had tears in her eyes. She wiped them away and looked at me.

"Looks like you might need some help here with a jump, you think?" I asked her.

"Oh god, I need help alright," she said. "I have got to get home and I have to get Alice to day care and I have to get to work somehow."

"Well, let me go get my car," I said. "I've got jumper cables and we'll see if we can get this here old girl started, OK?"

I went and got my car and pulled it up next to hers. There was no one parked in front of her, so I nosed on up in front of hers. I raised my hood and put on the jumper cables. I told her that we needed to give it a few minutes to let her battery charge up a bit before, we tried to start it.

So, while my car was idling, I got to find out a few things about her. Her name was Kathy. She was 24 years old. Alice's dad up and left there about 10 months ago and she has had a hard sledding ever since.

She got a job at Mission Linen Supply and it took all she made to pay the rent and day care. All said and done, her and Alice were just getting by.

"OK, try it now," I said.

She turned the key and tried to crank it up; no good. I let her know that we needed to let it charge up a bit more. Little Alice was sitting in the car seat in the back and looking at her mother.

"It's going to be alright, honey," I told her. "We're going to get you home safe and sound."

She looked at me and gave me a great big smile. In about 7 or 8 minutes I asked her to try it again and she cranked it over and it started!

"Let it warm up a bit, before you take off," I told her. "I'm going to follow you home to make sure that you get there safe. OK?"

I took off the jumpers, put them in my trunk, put both hoods down. I backed up enough to let her pull out and she did. There was smoke a plenty coming out of her tail pipe. She got going and I flipped a U turn and got behind her. She did not live too far from the park, maybe two miles or so. We were there in no time at all.

Her place was a pretty rundown apartment complex and she pulled into space #7 and I parked on the street.

I got out of my car and walked up to hers. I asked her to try and start it one more time. She did and it started!

I let her know that if it does not start in the morning to give me a call. I found a piece of paper in my wallet and got my pen out and gave her my cell phone number.

She thanked me and said that she may have to call me if it doesn't start again. She let me know that she can't afford to lose her job and her boss is not the most understanding person to work for. I let her know that was no problem and that I was on vacation and that I was an early riser.

I got back in the car, checked the address on the manager's door and then, I headed back to my motel room for an afternoon nap. That night, I lay in bed thinking about Kathy and her worn out old Chevy and things being so rough for her at this time. I'm going to see that she gets a good reliable car. She was going to be Robin Hood's first customer. Yea, this was a good thing. With a smile on my face, I drifted off to sleep.

The next morning, I was back at the same restaurant, the one I ate at the morning before. Having eggs and ham again, I like eggs and ham, topped that off with coffee and I was ready for anything that came down the pike.

Getting in my car, I looked in my back seat. Yep, there was that Teddy Bear sitting in the back quiet as could be. I had forgotten to give it to Alice. What did she say the name of her Teddy Bear friend was? Billy Boy, that was it!

This idea hit me and it made me grin. I wonder if this town had a shop that printed names, designs etc. on T-shirts.

Well one way to find out was to ask someone. I drove until, I see a woman's clothing store and pulled over and parked. I took old Billy Boy out of the back seat, put him under my right arm and then, I entered the shop. A nice woman caught my eye and I asked her if they have a store that does imprints on shirts. She smiled and told A nice woman caught my eye and I asked her if they have a store that does imprints on shirts. She smiled and told me that they do! She let me know that it was right down the street at 300 Koster. I got back in my car and drove to the store.

The shop was empty of people except for the man behind the counter. There was T-shirts on the display all over and they had baseball caps with all different sayings all over them.

"Can I help you," said the man.

"I sure hope so," I replied. "Billy Boy here needs about 3 T-shirts. Do you think you can fix us up?"

"What would you like printed on them," he asked.

"Well, let's see," I replied. "We want Billy Boy printed on them and right underneath that put "Alice's Best Friend". You think you can handle that?"

He laughed and said, "That's what we do here. We can fix you right up!"

So, when I left that shop, Billy Boy was wearing a green T-shirt with black printing of "Billy Boy, Alice's Best Friend".

He was looking good. I put him and the spare t-shirts in the back seat and told him to keep quiet and we took off. I was in a hell of a good mood. Me and Billy Boy was off to buy a car.

Sacramento has plenty of used car lots and it was no time at all I found plenty of cars to look at. I spent the morning strolling through car lots looking at all different kinds of cars. I wound up at Jim's Used Cars.

After looking through the lot at a lot of cars, which I know nothing about, this guy who had been standing aside watching me finely came up to me.

"I can see you are checking out our inventory of our fine cars here," he said. "Hi, I'm Jim Nelson, I'm the owner and Sales Manager. Can I ask what type of vehicle you are looking for?"

"Why yes," I said while grasping his hand and shaking it. "I'm R.J Hood and I'm looking for a Mini Van."

"What price range are you looking at?" he asked me.

"Oh about $6,000," I said.

"Well, we have three Mini Vans here for you to take a look at," he replied.

He took me and showed me a 2004 Suzuki 6 cylinder for $5,500. Then a Dodge Caravan 6 cylinder. It had a $6,500 price tag on the windshield.

"Can I take this one for a spin?" I asked about the Dodge Caravan.

"You sure can!" he replied. "Let me go grab the keys out of the office."

I don't know that much about cars, so I have to just go on feelings when it comes to buying one. He got the keys, raised the hood and checked the oil.

He showed me how clean the oil was. Told me about a few other things which, I knew nothing about. I didn't let on that I didn't know. He took the price tag off the windshield and threw it in the back seat. He climbed in the passenger seat and I got in and he handed me the keys.

I started it up and let it warm up a bit. Then, we were off! To make a short story about it, it ran real good, had plenty of pep and handled real good on the road. I liked it. So, when we got back to the lot, I told Jim that I was planning on buying it. We went into his office and he got the paperwork out and he put it on his desk.

I said, "Before you get the paperwork started, I'm going to tell you what I want to do, OK?"

He gave me a pretty funny look then, said, "OK."

"I'm going to pay cash for this car. I want two years of insurance on it. If anything breaks down in that two years, I want it covered, OK?" I told him.

"Another thing, this rig is not for me. It is for a young lady who lives here in your fair city. I want the pink slip in her name. So, are we on the same page?"

"Well, yea, Mr. Hood," he answered. "The final tally will be a little bit more, but we're on the same page."

"Now," I said. "I don't want her to know that I'm buying this for her. I want you to call her up, after 5:30 pm, because she works five days a week at Mission Linen. So, have her come down here and sign the papers and all that's needed to be done, OK? She has a clunker that might not ever make it here. You may have to go get her and bring her to the lot."

He did some figuring and then he told me that it would be a grand total of $7,857 and asked if we were still on the same page. I replied by peeling off the bills from one of the rolls of cash and gave him Kathy's name and address.

He got out the phone book and found her name in it. It was about 5 pm. She would be home in a half an hour if all went well.

"I'm going out to my car to get something. Give me the keys to the Caravan. I want to put something in the backseat for her daughter, OK?"

I went out to my car, grabbed Billy Boy and two extra T-shirts and went to the Caravan, put Billy Boy in the back seat and buckled him into the safety belt. I told him to hang on that his best friend was on her way.

I locked the van and headed back to Jim's office. He was hanging up his phone. I guess that she wasn't home, yet. Jim and I had a cup of coffee and then he tried again. This time she was there. Then, the fun began.

"Hello, Mrs. Martin?" he asked over the phone.

"Yes," she replied.

"This is Jim Nelson down here at Jim's used cars. I have a 2005 Dodge Caravan down here on my lot waiting for you to come and pick up and take home.

All you have to do is sign some paperwork, OK?" Jim said and waited for her response. I could not hear her but, knew she must be a bit confused.

"No, it's all paid for. All you have to do is put it in your name. No Mrs. Martin, this is not joke. If you think your car is not good enough to make it here, I'll come get you, OK? This is no joke played on you Mrs. Martin."

"Please, believe me. I'll be right here waiting for you." He gave her the address and then he hung up.

"I hope that she believes me enough to come down here," he said to me.

I said, "I'm going to sit in my car. It shouldn't take her long to get here, if her car will start. You'll haul it off to get rid of it won't you?"

"We'll handle it Mr. Hood. Don't you worry about it," he assured me.

I went out to my car and got in and waited to see if Kathy was going to show up. Sure enough, about 25 minutes later I see this cloud of smoke approaching the car lot. It was Kathy and little Alice. She came to a stop, got out and opened the back door to let Alice out onto the car lot. Jim was right on the ball and came trotting out of his office.

"Mrs. Martin, I hope," Jim said.

"Yes, I'm Kathy Martin," she replied. "This had better not be a joke."

"This is no joke," Jim said. "You follow me and I'll show you your van."

I had gotten out of my car trying to stay out of sight and followed up at a distance. Jim took them over to the van and unlocked it. Little Alice was right on her mother's heels. Jim opened the driver's door then, seen what was in the back seat and then went around and opened the right rear door. I told Jim about Alice and he played his part well.

"Come over here, Alice," Jim told her. "I have something to show you."

Alice came around and looked in the door. She saw the Teddy Bear!

"Billy Boy!" she shouted. "Mamma it's Billy Boy. Look!"

My heart sang. She was one happy little girl, let me tell you! I eased on back to my car then, headed back to my motel room. Robin Hood was feeling good! I found me a nice little Italian restaurant and had me a good meal.

Then, I drove over to Kathy's place. There in parking space #7 sat a pretty little 2005 Dodge Caravan looking right at home. I just cruised on by. I seen what I came to see. I headed for my room. Us old codgers have got to get our rest.

That night I ran through my mind all that transpired up to this day. I could have bought Kathy a brand new one, but wanted to her to feel that she had gotten a helping hand and that she had to keep on bettering herself.

From what I had found out about her, I think I had her figured out just about right. Well, time will tell. I was the one who was dolling out this money and I would decide who and how much.

So far, I had real good feelings about the way things were going. My work, if you wanted to call it that was done here in Sacramento. I was going to head out for new country. Right now, Mr. Robin Hood needs a good night's sleep and see what tomorrow brings.

I slept in the next morning or at least tried to. I had me breakfast at a different restaurant. I was starting to get bold, now. I even ordered an omelet. That was really different for me. I had just a couple of stops, before I left town.

First, I stopped at Jim Nelson's Car Lot. Jim was there and was not busy. I waved and he came over to me.

"Hello, Mr. Hood," Jim said. "Your girl got her van and was so very happy. Little Alice was just like you told me. She had the biggest smile ever."

"Jim, I came by before I left town to thank you on how you handled the van deal," I told him. "You went beyond what was called for. Especially, when you spotted that bear in the back seat. Getting that bear made her just beam. You're a good man, sir. I took out 3 $100 bills and handed them to him. Jim, you take care!"

I got in my car to go to my last stop, before I left town. I arrived at Kathy's place a few minutes later. I knew she was at work and Little Alice at Day Care. I had written a short letter, before I went to bed last night.

Dear Kathy,

you are probably wondering what has happened to you in the last few days and why it happened. Don't try and figure it out, just do me this one favor, keep doing your best. Don't give up on life. You have yourself a beautiful daughter. That's reason enough to keep going. Here's a little more help with the bills etc. (I had put 40 $100 bills in with the letter) I will be checking later on to see how you are getting along. Try and stay in a positive frame of. Sincerely, R. Hood

I placed the envelope through the mail slot in the door. I got back in my little red car and started leaving Sacramento California heading South on the I-5. The radio was playing some Country music and I tuned in while the tires were humming in my little car.

My mind was turning from one thing to another. Then, I just started laughing and for a while, I just could not stop laughing. I felt like a thief making his getaway. I still felt funny about the money, but as time passed, it got easier and easier to live with.

I left most of the money back at the apartment. I brought $250,000 with me on the first trip. I started laughing, again thinking a 1/4 of a million dollars was enough for an old sod like me to deal with right now. Before I left Eureka, I was given this money belt from a friend who told me jokingly if I was ever to come into some money and tool a trip it could come in handy if I was in need of some fast cash money. Well, my belt had 2 grand in it and the rest was in the trunk down where I kept the spare tire. My wallet had about 5-6 hundred in it, so I wouldn't feel bad when I opened it up! Mr. R Hood was dialed in, feeling good and moving on or so I thought.

Robin Hood Leaves Sacramento

Heading south on the I-5, I was trying to hold my speed at 65 and keep over on the far-right lane. I watched for cars and trucks and whatever sailed past me as if I was standing still. My mind began to wonder. It's been known to do so every so often. I wondered how my friends were doing back in Eureka. Were they treating Patrick the way they were supposed to? Was the

The Club running the way it should? Then, I had a good laugh. Hell, I was acting like this old world will not run without me! You had better decide where you're going to! If you keep heading south, you're going to end up on Mexico and you don't want to end up there!

It wasn't long, before I seen a sign saying, "275 East". Then, "58 East" to Bakersfield. I knew then, I would not end up in Mexico and started feeling better. A growl started in my old gut and knew that I needed to stop and eat pretty soon! I was getting close to Barstow and I figured that would be a good enough place to fill up my car and myself.

I found a truck stop, filled up my little red girl with gas and then, went in to the restaurant of the truck stop to take care of that growl in my stomach I was telling you about. A gal about 45 or 50, I've never been good at guessing ages, came up to me.

"Hello handsome," she said to me.

She had one hell of a good smile and handed me a menu, winked at me and left. I couldn't remember the last time that I have been called handsome, but it was a long time ago! So, I ate me a good meal, tipped that big chested, big smiling waitress and got directed to a Motel 6 where they kept the light on for me and called it a night.

Up early, I opened the blinds to see of my car was still outside. No reason in the world it wouldn't be, but no harm in checking! They had a coffee maker on the room. It was kind of like a little Mr. Coffee maker and packaged up for one or two cups; wasn't that bad.

After belting down a couple, I was ready to hit the road. I wasn't hungry. I thought I'd eat a little down the line.

I was getting close to Arizona somewhere around Needles. Radio playing and the weather was nice. I was heading back north and then east on highway 40. It was leading to where I didn't know, but this fine day, I was on my way. I guess it was close to Kingman, when I seen him. He was on the on ramp. He had a long coat on and like a wide brimmed leather fedora hat on.

I pulled off and stopped thinking I could use a little company right about now. I watched him trot up to the car in my rear-view mirror.

Benny Luna

When he got close, I opened the passenger side, so he could climb in. He got to the passenger door, took off his long coat and hat and then, got in.

"Throw your coat and hat in the back seat if you want to," I told him.

He did just that, took a large breath and smiled at me. Then, settled back in his seat.

"Ben Luna," he said to me sticking out his hand. "I thank you for the ride and yes, it's been about 3 hours since the last ride."

That was my first introduction to Benny Luna an Indian like no other Indian I had ever met. I didn't know it then, but my life made a change after that meeting. My outlook on life made a change after that; my outlook on life and a few other things. I just did not know it at the time. I glanced over at him seeing a man of about 40 years. He had a necklace hanging from his neck; a beautiful silver and turquoise with Indian markings on it. His hat that I thought looked like a Fedora had a hat band on it with Indian markings on it. Yep, I had me a real live Indian ridding in my little red Ford Focus!

"Where you going to, if I may ask," I said to him.

"I'm going home to my people," he replied. "I've have been on a road to hell and it's time I went home to right a few wrongs. God knows, I have a lot of them."

I pulled back on the highway and headed east. Little by little I got Ben or Benny as he began talking about himself and his life.

"I was born on the Navajo Nation on a place called Ya-Ta-Hey," he began to tell me. "It is a place a few miles north of Gallup, New Mexico. The year was 1956. When I was six, I rode along with the kids on an old school bus into Gallup to go to the first grade. I knew right from the start that I was different. The White man's world was not for me and my own people. I felt that I didn't fit with them either. I felt like I was an outsider in both worlds."

I could tell that he trusted me and that he needed to get a lot off his chest. That's what we do in AA, no matter if they are an alcoholic or not, we try and place others first. I just drove and listened to his life story.

"By the time I was in 3rd grade, I started skipping school. I would hide out until, it was time to catch the bus back home. Well, that did not last and when my Dad found out what was going on, he took the belt to me.

"My Dad was Old School. He believed in the phrase, "Spare the Rod, spoil the child." He literally beat the hell out of me. I stopped skipping school, but I refused to learn. I would just sit back in class and stare out the window."

"So, I passed each grade with a D – average. They just moved me up with the lowest one can pass a grade. It was 1965. I got off the school bus that brought me home from school. My mother was at the kitchen table, head bent and quietly sobbing. I asked her what was wrong."

"That is when I found out that my father had been killed by a drunk driver. My Dad was a mailman. He was hit crossing 9th street in Gallup. He was taken to the hospital, but died on the way."

"My mother fell apart. She was never the same after that. She withdrew from life and turned to the bottle. My life changed also. I didn't have anyone make me behave myself and I must say that I took advantage of that situation."

"Reform school was where I wound up. A young Indian boy with a belly full of hate heading for hell. I struggled on. Then, in 1974, I was in Germany in the U.S. Army. I came back to the states to finish up my Army time at Ft. Lewis in Washington then, headed home to Gallup. They taught me how to drive a truck in the army. So, when I came home, I lucked out and got me a job delivering auto parts. It didn't pay a lot, but it got me by.

Then, in the summer of 1978, I was at the Inter-Tribal Ceremonial. That was where the Navajo-Zuni-Hopi and Acoma tribes could come together and share in Indian culture of all the surrounding tribes. That is when I met the woman that would become my wife and give me my one and only son."

"She came to Redrock Park with some of her people who came to share some of their dances with the rest of the tribes. I was standing at a booth waiting to get some juice to drink with some ice."

"She stepped up to the booth and gave me that sweet wonderful smile that I would fall in love with. We introduced ourselves. I asked her for her phone number and she gave it to me!"

"After the tribal get together was over, I got to calling her in the evenings after work. There we were, a Zuni maiden and a lost and lonely Navajo warrior, if you could call me that. Lost and lonely I was dead on the mark. Marie filled that emptiness inside of me. For the first time that I can remember, I was happy.

That was when I found out that I had a singing heart, when I was with Marie. White men might say, "You're just crazy in love". I guess that I was. There are two sides to the story. Marie took a liking to this crazy Navajo and that we would get married and start us a family. So, that is what we did."

"Things went along good at first. Marie was a good and loyal wife; faithful. She kept the house clean, fed me and did all the things a wife should do. "

"The problems that started to crop up had to do with me. Let me say right up front. It was me that tore our lives apart. It started off slowly at first; just a few beers after work, so I could unwind."

"I did alright with it for the first few years. At least I thought I was doing alright. Looking back on it now, I can see how the booze was changing our lives."

"Our son, Danny was born early in our marriage. He is a beautiful boy with long legs like his Dad. Marie had her hands full with a baby and me. My Navajo elders had given up on me years ago. I did not and would not listen to the wise men of my tribe. I had something inside me. I had a hate and fear that would every so often come out in anger and people just got away from me. I had an evil spirit in me that was like a cancer and it slowly was eating me up.

"The years went by and my drinking progressed right up until, I had the reek of booze in my truck. By that time, I was drinking on the job and was drinking every day."

"To make a long story short, "They" meaning the law, handcuffed me and threw me in the back of a police car and hauled me off to jail. I was in jail for two days."

"When I got out, my boss told me my truck driving days were over. That I was fired and to get the hell off the company property!"

I had to go to court for what I had done a few days earlier. I got fined, which I refused to pay, so I spent the next 36 days in jail. That is the way it went for me. I had become a "Hang Out' down by the train tracks. I did not live at home anymore. I had no home. I only went to Marie's to get a ten spot or a twenty to help me get through another hell ridden day. Marie had went and got herself a job. She could no longer count on me. "

"The last memory I have of Marie and my son, Danny was the deep hurt in her eyes and the disgust and anger in my son's eyes. That is when I made up my mind to leave. I had nothing to give anyone. All I had was emptiness and a deep sickness in my soul.

I knew that before I caused any more hurt, I had best leave right away. So, I caught a freight train west and that is how I wound up in California.

"I moved around a lot. I worked in the fields picking apples, worked in the grape fields and worked when and where I could. Most all of my money went to booze. I went to temporary work agencies for day labor."

"I worked when I had to and only if I had to. I was in a downward spiral. I still went to jail every once in a while, for drunk in public, but for the most part, I learned how to get away from the law."

"My world became a gray haze and living hell. I moved around a lot not getting to know people or letting them get to know me. I liked it like that. At least I told myself I did. I started having black outs. I could not remember and they kept getting longer and longer. I would come to and not remember where I was.

I would get D.T.'s seeing things that were not there; hallucinations. I thought that people were after me! There were grave emotional and mental disorders inside this Navajo. I was at my end."

That is when God sent a man who took this shell of a man and started me on this new path that I am on now. Mitch was the man's name. He was a little fella in stature. He had a bushy beard on his face. He kind of looked like Gabby Hayes in them old western movies. I was on a back street in the town of Barstow in an alley way right close to a dumpster sitting down on some card board boxes. I was leaning against the backside of an old building with a bottle of port wine inside of a brown paper bag tucked in my beat-up old trench coat.

The bottle was almost empty as it always seems to be with me. I never had enough; almost out, that was me. I was drifting in and out of my childhood times. Some good and some, not so good. I was in a gray hazy state of mind when, I heard this voice saying, 'Hey you, over there! Are you OK?'"

"I did not know if this voice was from inside my head or not. Then, I heard it again. This voice saying, 'What the hell are you doing in this fancy little alley way!' "I raised my head and saw this little guy with a fuzzy beard, skinny as a rail. 'A hell of a place for a man like you to be hanging out at.'

I asked him what the hell he wanted and to mind his own damn business. He says to me that he could be doing that, but he has been looking all over town to find the right man to share this bowl of stew with. He let me know that he hated eating alone. Sick as I was, I had to laugh.

He laughed too! He told me that he has been told that he makes a damn good pot of beef stew and asked me if I would like to go to his place to find out if that is true about his stew!"

"I don't remember much about that day, but I know that it was the day that I met Mitch! I did not know it at that time, but that was the day my life began to change. Mitch took me over to his place and I tried to eat some of his stew.

I cannot remember if I was able to or not, but I do remember that he offered me a place to stay for a few days. He had an old tool shed in the back. "

"There was a cot with a sleeping bag and a pillow. In the corner was a toilet. Mitch told me if I wanted to stop living the way I had been living and start a new one, he would help me.

He also told me he had met many a bullshitter and con man and that he would soon find out if I was one of them or not. He also told me that it would not be easy and that I would be going through hell for three or four days. He let me know that if I wanted to change my life for the better, we could start right then and there."

"He would stay right there with me until, I got through those first few days and thank god he did. It was utter hell! Mitch weened me off the wine. Every hour he would give me a little glass of wine. He kept cutting back on the amount. I remember begging him for more, but he kept letting me know that I was going to make it through. He stayed with me until, I fell asleep."

"When I woke up, he was right there beside me. I did not drink any more wine. I was sick as hell, but I hung on and ever so slowly I got better. I was able to get down some of Mitch's beef stew. Mitch may have made a good stew, but had to be the world's worst coffee maker. But right about then, I was grateful to be alive and been through that hell I had been in."

"Mitch sat me down, looked me straight in the eyes and told me, 'You are in the right place in your life that you have to make a decision right here and now. Are you going to go back to that shit of a life you were in or are you willing to change to something new and better?'"

"Well, I went for hanging with Mitch. He started taking me to AA meetings and to the Salvation Army to get clothes to wear. Each day, I got a little healthier and stronger. Mitch told me I was not nothing but, that I was something that came from God and God did not make junk. I was worthy of having a good life. If I did a few simple things and if I was sincere, my life would turn around for the better. Well, I bought into that and Mitch became the first white man I have ever loved. He told me the truth, even if it pissed me off and a lot of times it did."

"For the first time I can remember, I started living my life on honest principles. Mitch and I made a deal with each other. We would not lie to each other, no matter what! Mitch had been living that way for years, but I was just starting out on this new way of life."

"He asked straight out, 'What do you wanna do with your life?'"

"I had been thinking about this for a while and so I replied, 'For myself, I want nothing, but for my wife and son, I want to help them anyway that I can. I know they probably don't want anything to do with me now, but if I can help them in anything, that is what I wish to do with my life."

'Well, you start off by taking care of yourself first,' Mitch told me. 'To do that, you got to get and stay sober. You need to change from the inside out.'"

"So, my new life began one day at a time. I woke up early every morning and had breakfast with Mitch. Then, we would head off to an AA meeting. It was not long until, I got a job working for a janitorial service. It seems that Mitch knew a hell of a lot of people of all kinds. He introduced me to Jeff, who owned the janitorial company.

Jeff put me to work on a trial basis. I wasn't about to let Mitch down, so I went to work every day and gave a good day's work for a good day's pay."

"My life got better with each passing day. I got me a room downtown when, I had a couple of three pay days. You see, Mitch wanted that cot in his shed in case another crazy Indian might come into town in the same condition I was in. You can guess that Mitch has helped more than one drunk get off the street and back on his feet and into life.

"So, you see Mister, that is why I am going home," Benny told me. "I'm going to face the music. I don't expect my wife or son will be welcoming me back. The time has come to try and help them in any way I can."

I was touched by his story. I could feel the sincerity coming out of him. I sure as hell knew what he went through with his drinking problem.

All I had to do was think back on my drinking years.

I looked over to the passenger seat and took a good look at who was riding with me. I saw a clear-eyed man who had purpose in his life. He looked nothing like that drinking Indian who left New Mexico like the one in the story he just got through telling me about. No, this was not that same man.

"How about us pulling off and getting some food inside us?" I asked him. "I'm starting to get hungry."

Needles Arizona

We were coming up on the Arizona border so, when we got to Needles, I took the first exit and stopped at the first place that came to us. It was a little hamburger joint.

It had three tables with umbrellas in the middle of the tables outside. We got a couple of hamburgers with fries and a soda. Ben, who I soon got to calling Benny asked me what I was doing and where was I going. I thought for a moment and then, started to laugh. I could not tell him that I was going around the country giving money away to people. I thought I needed a story to tell others. I told him that I was on vacation with no certain place to go in mind. Benny told me that was the best vacation to be on! Benny was easy to talk to and one felt good to be in his company. We finished eating.

Benny offered to pay for our meal. I told him if he didn't mind that I would take care of it and that I needed to spend some of my vacation money. I had already paid, when he went to the bathroom. His offering told me a little of himself; he was not a bum.

We loaded up in my little red Ford and was soon back on the road headed northeast toward Kingman. There we went, one old worn out logger and an Indian who is trying to get home and make things right with his family.

I have always been a good listener when people talk and had a knack at asking the right questions at the right time.

Most people seem to trust me and will open up and share some of their inner most thoughts. Not all of them do, but most do. So, it was with Benny, I could see that he was a man on a mission and was not going to let anything stop him, no matter how long it took. I got quiet for a while and I thought that Benny might have dropped off to sleep, but he told me a saying I hope that I never forget.

"Come what may, hold fast to love. Though men may bend your heart, let them not embitter or harden it. We win by tenderness. We conquer by forgiveness."

Wow, I thought what a saying coming out of an Indian named Benny. There is a hell of lot more to this man than meets the eye. I knew then and there that I had to get to know him better. There is dam few people that I feel that way about and I was adding Benny to that list.

Gallup, New Mexico

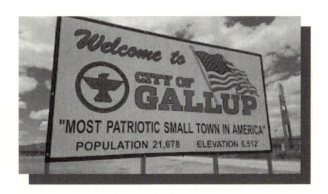

We came into Gallup late in the evening. I suggested to Benny that we get a motel room and that we would figure out what we would do the next morning. Benny was tired and didn't say no. I spotted a Motel 6, pulled in and got us each a room. I told Benny I would see him in the morning, took a hot shower and hit the sack. I slept soundly.

The next thing I knew, it was morning. I got dressed, went to the door and looked outside. There was Benny standing not far from my door.

"Hey Benny," I said. "Good morning! Why didn't you knock on my door?"

"I thought you might need your sleep," he told me. "I see that you're an early riser also."

"Yea, I am," I replied. "Let's go find us some food, so we can start this day off the right way. OK?"

Benny grinned and replied," Lead on my good man. Lead on!"

We found a Denny's there on route 66. We went in and got a booth. A waitress brought us some coffee, took our order and left us sitting there across from each other waiting for the other to talk. Finely, it was I who spoke.

"Well Benny, where are you going from here?" I asked him. "You have any plans on what you are going to do next?"

"Yes, I have a cousin here in Gallup who told me he would put me up for a few days, if I didn't drink and didn't cause him or his family any trouble," he said. "You know how it is with people like us!"

The waitress brought us our breakfast and we both dove in.

"I think I might stay here in Gallup for a few days and see what life was like here in the high desert," I told him. "How bout we find us a meeting to go to here in Gallup?"

"I was hoping you would say that," Benny replied.

I let him know that I'd never been to an AA meeting in New Mexico. He laughed and let me know that he hadn't either. So after breakfast, Benny called his cousin and got the address of the nearest AA meeting. The name of the group there was called, "Wings of the Storm". It was across from the train station on 1st Street.

The man who was running the meeting was standing outside smoking, when we pulled up and parked.

His name was Steve. As we walked up to him, I asked, "Is this the place where people come to that have a problem when they consume alcohol?"

He let out a laugh and said, "By God, you got it on the first try. Welcome! I got the coffee on the making right now and the meeting will be starting in about a half hour."

We introduced ourselves. Benny asked about a few people he knew, before he left for

California. Steve knew a few of them. In fact, a couple of them came to the meeting. We were shooting the breeze, when this Indian fella walked up to us and grabbed Benny, swung him around and slapping him on the back making a hell of a lot of noise! Then, things settled down.

"John, you know that cousin I was telling you about?" Benny asked me.

"Well, here he is. John, this is my cousin, Stubby Luna. Most people call him, Stub."

We shook hands, then went inside, got us some coffee, got us a seat and settled in for a meeting. As the meeting was going on, I got to thinking how God works in strange ways sometimes.

Here, I bring this Indian all the way from California and one of the first people we meet is the one who he is going to stay with and they both belong to the same fellowship! When the meeting was over, Benny and Stubby came over to the table Steve and I was sitting at.

"John, I thank you for the ride home and the other things you did for me," Benny said to me. "I will be leaving with Stub. I hope to see you around here for a while. It's been nice."

"Thanks, Benny. It's nice of you to say that and yes, I plan on staying a while here." I answered.

I gave Benny my cell phone number and he gave me Stub's home phone number. We said our good byes and the next thing I knew, it was just Steve and I left in the meeting.

"Well now, California," Steve said to me. "How bout you and I straighten up this place, closing up shop and going over to my place. That is, if you have nothing better to do?"

With nothing better to do, we did just that. Steve lived in Gamerco. It had nothing more than a post office and service station. I got some much-needed rest in Gamerco by staying in Steve's spare room and going to meetings.

I got a call from my niece and she told me that my brother had died from his long bout with cancer. I let her know that I would be back in the area in a bit and call me when the funeral arrangements are made and I would be there.

I said my good byes to Steve, Benny and the folks I met in Gamerco. I let Benny know that I would be in touch with him after letting him know of my brother's death. I left Benny $2,500 to help pay his wife back for the money he got from her for alcohol in his hard times.

I got my car gassed up and headed back to Eureka. It was a 1,200-mile drive and I wanted to make sure that I was back in the area for my brother's funeral, so I made it to Bakersfield and got a room at a hotel. I got up with the sun and made it to Eureka as the sunset.

I pulled into my parking space, went upstairs and into my apartment. Everything looked just like I left it. I saw my Lazy Boy chair waiting for me. I went to it, thinking about what I was going to do next.

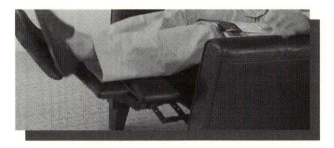

It felt good being back home sitting in my Lazy Boy, but that was only part of it. It felt good being home in Eureka among my people.

I remember back 35 years ago, a man who was so empty and lost, not knowing where to turn to and then, being taken into the fellowship of A.A. I thought to myself, 'Yes John, you are a lucky man and you had better not forget that.'

Then, putting on some coffee and I go into the bedroom, open the clothes closet, grab the laundry bag, toss it up on the bed and out rolls the money I left behind when I went off on my little venture. So, I put the bills back in the laundry bag, $597,000 and put it back in the closet. Back to the kitchen and I grab my favorite cup and pour me some "Joe" and get back in my lazy boy.

'Yeah, it sure is nice to be home. That feeling that I belong came over me sitting in my chair that fit my butt only from all the times I used it.'

The next morning, I enter The Club seeing that Illeane was working the counter that day. She gave me a smile.

"I suppose you would like some coffee, John," she said to me.

"Yep, I sure would," I answered.

After getting my coffee, I went over to the round table and took a seat. I was early and the only other person at the table was Mike. He was just in for a quick cup, before heading to work.

Hey John," he said to me. "Glad to see that you are back. I'd like to stay and chat, but I got to get an early start and take down a few trees. Gotta go!"

As he was heading out, in came Patrick and he went up to the counter and Illeane poured him some coffee. He saw me and a grin came on his face.

"Hi, John," he said. "Where you been? I haven't seen you for a long time."

"I've been on vacation, Patrick," I replied. " I had to come back and take car of some business.

I had learned to keep things light, when it came to talking to Patrick.

"They been treating you alright while I've been gone?" I asked him.

"Yeah," he replied. "I got to go walk, John. I got to go walk."

He fixed his coffee and headed out. Then, in came Bill; my little buddy who I liked to joke with. I would ask him to tell his wife that I send my best and also, he better treat her good.

The Club was starting to fill up for the morning meeting. Sitting at the round table, I got this feeling how lucky I was. A lot of Newcomers that wasn't here the last time I was home. One thing about this outfit I belong to, we never run out of new people.

Then, comes in my best friend Fred. It felt good seeing him again and that friendly smile he brought with him.

"Hello John. It's good to have you back home. "We got a lot to talk about."

I told him about my brother Jim, but kept it very light about my trip. I got around to asking about what was happening in Eureka.

Robin Hood Saves

The Club

"Well, John," Fred said. "You are going to hear about this anyway, so might I might as well tell you now. We are out of here in 60 days. I don't know if they're selling the building or just what the hell is happening. I just know that they told us we got to leave here in two months. I know that this is going to piss you off, but what the hell can we do about it?"

"Well, Fred," I said. "It does upset me about The Club."

My mind started racing and I had to tell myself to slow down then, start thinking about what should be done about this problem. Right off my mind went to the money in my closet and in the trunk of my little Ford Focus. How can I get some of it and a new place for The Club that will help the people who I care so deeply about? I know that I don't want to get into trouble with the law over this. I know that I'm still not going to take that money down to the police station. Oh well, I got 60 days to work on this.

One thing I know is that, I don't know how I'm going to figure this out. I know that I am going to have to get help figuring this out because, I'm not smart enough to do this on my own. That night sitting in my thinking chair, my mind went to Kathy in Sacramento. I was wondering how she and little Alice was doing. So, I called and sure enough Kathy picked up on the other end.

"Hello, Kathy," I said. "How are you and little Alice getting along? This is R. Hood. I told you I would be checking up on you so, that's what I'm doing."

"Glad to hear from you Mr. Hood," Kathy replied. "Things are a lot different than they were when, we first met. I have not been late going to work one time, since I got my new car. I know it's not brand new, but it's new to me. The best vehicle I have ever owned. Now for Alice, she is growing like a weed. She started wearing those T-shirts you gave her for Billy Boy. Her Billy Boy said he would share them with her. As for me, I've met a nice guy. He's a lineman for the phone company. I'm quite taken with him.

But after Robert, Alice's dad left us, I'm not leaping into another relationship. So, I'm taking it slow. One thing in his favor, Alice really likes him and he is quite taken with her. That is very important to me. I don't want her hurt again. So,

Mr. Hood, that's how things are on this end. How are things going for you?"

I told her things were fine in my life. I did not want to pull her hopes and dreams down. It did bring a smile to my face. I felt good inside and it all started from a beautiful little girl staring at me in a park in Sacramento. Do you know that wonderful feeling deep inside you get when no one, but God and you know that you did something good and that you want to keep on doing it? Well, that is what I'm feeling and I'm going to hang on to this as long as I can.

I went to bed and slept like a little baby that had been given a Teddy Bear. The next morning, I came into The Club with a purpose. I had been thinking on how to keep The Club going and I think I had it almost figured out. I got my coffee, went to the round table and then, went into deep thinking mode where I started talking to myself. I try not to do it out loud.

'John, you're an alcoholic, aren't you? Yep, I sure am! I believe you belong to this outfit called Alcoholics Anonymous, right? Right again! Well, why don't you give a certain amount each month to The Club anonymously?

Then, I ask myself, 'Can I do that? Why in the hell not! I need to find one person who I could trust with the money for The Club. Who loves The Club as much as I do? Well, I have been around quite a few years and I think I have learned a few things and became a pretty good judge of people. I believe I was looking at him that morning. James was working the counter. He seemed to be doing that more and more these days.

James was honest, always there when The Club needed help, but most of all, he cared and it showed time after time. He never bragged about helping out, he just did it and kept quiet about it. Yes, I believe James is the man I want to talk about this with, so I walked over to him when he was alone at the counter.

"James, what are you doing after you close up The Club?" I asked him.

Well, John," he replied. "I have a few "Honey Do's at the house that the little woman wants me to do. What do you have in mind?"

"James, I want to talk to you about something that I believe is important to both of us," I told him.

"Well, John," he replied. "Can we do this tomorrow morning?"

"OK, tomorrow morning it is," I replied to him. "We'll have breakfast and I'm buying, OK? We'll talk about that tomorrow morning."

The next morning, I took in a meeting. Then, went into The Club room where once again James was working the counter.

"You still want to go for breakfast this morning, John," James asked me.

"That's why I'm here," I replied. "You want to go to Adel's?"

I knew that it was one of his favorite places for breakfast or lunch. When he started shutting things down, he said, "You go ahead John, I'll see you down there OK?"

Down at Adel's, I got us a table and it was not long before, James came in. He seen where I was then, came over and joined me. We ordered our meal.

"What is it that is so important that you got to take your old buddy James out to breakfast for?

By the way, sorry to hear about your brother John."

"Thanks," I said. "When it's our time, it's our time and nothing we can do to change it. But what I want to talk to you about is about The Club. I hear we have to be out of there in 60 days. Is that right?"

"That's the word, John," James replied.

"Well, James," I am going to ask you a few questions and get your opinion, OK?" I told him.

"Alright, shoot!" said James.

"Do you trust me, James?" I asked him. "And do you believe me when, I'm not joking around?"

"Serious, John?" James told me. "All the time I've known you, I have found you to be good to your word. What you got to tell me, get it out so, we both know what the hell you're talking about."

"I found a benefactor for The Club," I told him. "When we find a new place to move into, the benefactor wants to remain anonymous so, I cannot tell you who it is. So, we are back to me. He will give us five thousand each month for a year and, if we do good, he said he will continue on, a year at a time basis. That way we can end up owning the building and never have to worry about getting kicked out again"

"Well John," he told me. "I believe you and I'll believe old Mr. Anonymous when, he forks over the money. I take it you want me to set this up and run it?"

"Yes, I do," I answered. "I'm asking you to believe me and to trust me to keep my word."

I stuck out my hand and James shook it. Then, my phone rang. It was my niece from Ft. Bragg.

"Hello Uncle John," she said. "This is Candy. Uncle Jim's funeral will be this Sunday. It will be a grave side service. So, I'll see you Sunday at eleven O'clock. He will be buried next to mom. I know you want to come."

John's Brother's Funeral

Sunday came and I went to Ft. Bragg to my brother Jim's funeral. The weather was fair and warm. Brother Jim had a lot more people come and pay their respects than I thought would attend. That made me feel good knowing that Jim had people that cared enough to send him off with kind words.

I was not among those that spoke. My words were said at the old home place, when I was here last. After thanking my niece for handling the funeral, I went over to my son, said my good byes and headed north to Eureka. It was good to be going back home, again.

That evening, I got a call from Mike that owned Mike's Tree Services.

"Hey John, we're looking for a speaker this coming month," Mike said to me. "Since you just got back, I thought you just might have come across someone on your trip who will be our next speaker for this coming month."

Right away, my mind went to Benny and told him about being the speaker for the upcoming month and would he think he would be willing to tell his story in front of a few people or should I say to a couple of hundred people? So I called Benny to ask him. He answered.

"Well, John it would be a first for me," Benny replied. "You have been so good to me with your help for me and my family that there is no way I could turn you down."

I didn't say anything knowing that all he would have to say is that he did not want to do that. But I was so very happy that he agreed to come to Eureka and tell his story. I told him the date of the speaker meeting. He asked for me to tell who ever asked him to speak that he'll be there to speak.

I phone back to Mike and told him to get ready for a Navajo Indian speaker next month.

He laughed and said, "Bring him on! And by the way, thank you."

Benny Makes Amends

Saturday morning on her day off from work sat Marie Luna staring into her coffee cup when, a quiet and gentle knock came on her front door. She opened it up about an inch or to see who was on the other side and there staring back at her was Benny.

She swung the door open and there in front of her was the man that she thought she had lost forever. She had been praying for him daily to get well and change his life. Standing there with nice clothes on and fresh new haircut. She looked into his eyes, they were clear and they were the eyes that she fell in love with many years ago.

"Marie would you give me a few minutes of time to talk to you this morning?" Benny asked her. "I won't take up too much of your time, but there are things I need to tell you."

"Yes, you may come in Benny," Marie answered." Danny stayed overnight at his friend's house last night and before you ask, I will tell you he is fine and in good health."

She offered him a cup of coffee, which he quickly accepted. They sat at her kitchen table and Benny spoke to her.

"Marie, I'm not here to beg your forgiveness or make you a lot of promises, but I'm here to ask you let me show you that I have changed from what I was and into the man I want to be," Benny gently told her. "Alcohol took me to a bad place in my life one day at a time. I'm on a path of recovery and it is a path I walk one day at a time. God has put people in my life to help show me the way forward. I would have never got to where I am today on my own.

May I never forget that because, if I do, I'll fall back into that alcohol hell. So, I am here to find out if I get that chance that I probably don't deserve and with that I wait for your reply."

"Benny, I must say that I was taken aback when you knocked on my door this morning," Marie replied. "I see that you're not the man I would let in the last time I saw you. No, there has been a change in you and for that my heart does rejoice. Many a night, I have laid in bed wondered if you were still alive and safe. I have loved you since we first met and I still do, but it's like a you say, this is going to be a one day at a time thing. I thank you for not pushing for us to get back together right now. This is going to take time for the both of us."

Standing in the shower after Benny had left with the water pouring over her it was one of the places she felt closest to God. This was such a time for her to speak to God.

"Thank you, my God. You have answered my prayer. You have kept Benny safe and brought him back home. So as he told me before left, 'One day at a time.'"

After showering and getting dressed she noticed Benny's coffee cup and under it was some bills. Picking up the cup, she saw that he had left four one hundred-dollar bills. She picked them up and leaned her head back and smiled. Then, said, 'God, I think the change in my life has started.'

Danny came home about 1 O'clock looking for something to eat. After giving his mother a hug and a kiss on the cheek, he sat down at the kitchen table. She fixed him two big sandwiches, a tall glass of milk and sat them in front of him.

"Son, I want to tell you something," his mother told him. "I had a visitor this morning and before you say anything, I want you to hear me out without any interruptions, OK?"

"OK," he replied.

"Your Dad came by. He was sober. He was clean and clear eyed. Now, wait," she told him holding up her hand. "I said to hear me out!" He did not ask for anything, only for the chance to prove that he has turned his life around."

"Well, that sounds pretty good," Danny replied. "But he's going to have to do a hell of a lot of proving to me before, I change my mind about him."

"Well son," his mother replied. "That is all that he is asking for and all that I'm asking is that you keep an open mind and that you be fair about this. OK?"

"OK, Mom," Danny said, "But I'm not going to take any more of what it was like when he was last here."

"Fair enough, son," Mom said. "I feel the same way as you do, but let's you and I give him a chance to prove himself. OK?"

"OK, Mom," Danny replied. "Oh yeah Mom, my buddy Sully said to tell you thank you for the cookies you gave him to take home and said they were better than the ones that his mother makes, but not to let her ever find out."

She tussled the top of his head knowing that he and Sully were off to do what all 15-year-old boys do. Yes, things had changed and for the better. Little did she know that in just a few short days that she would be leaving a place she has not traveled from more than 50 miles to a place where giant redwood trees grew and had lush mountains around them.

No, she did not know this, but her surprise was just around the corner. At that moment, she felt joy in her heart for what God had given her. She thanked Him again. Then, she started her day.

Benny and Marie to The Redwoods

It was three days away from the upcoming speaker meeting. Benny had called me and asked if it would be alright if he brought Marie, his wife with him. I laughed and said not only was it alright, but required. He said he didn't know for sure if she could get off work, but he believed she could. Said he would call the day before he arrived in Eureka.

Benny and his wife arrived at my place the day before, the speaker meeting. I got to meet Marie and soon found why Benny wanted her for his wife. She was so very real. Also, she was pleasant to be around; a good down to earth person. I asked if they wanted to rest up for a while or go down to the harbor and see the fishing boats then, go to a seafood restaurant and eat some of our famous seafood. They voted for the latter.

It was as if Marie turned into a little girl again. She was soon pointing at things and asking all kinds of questions. She got a kick out of watching the seagulls fly around and the dolphins bobbing around in the bay. When we went to the Cafe Marina on Woodley Island, I got a kick out of Marie trying to figure out what to order. I suggested she try a little of everything so she could find out what she liked best and that is what she did.

I kept watching Benny watching her and could see pride and happiness come out in him. The weather was fine and not too cold, so we sat at a table out on the deck where you could see the fishing boats better. It was something to see people see things for the first time. Having finished our meals and seeing a few yawns, I suggested we call it a day. So, we went back to my place and called it a night. I have a spare bedroom and I tried to see that they had everything they needed.

"Don't worry, John. We're fine," Marie told me.

Benny said that he was going to sleep on the couch and that was that! So, we finely went to bed. Up as early as I always do, I seen that I wasn't the first one up. There was Benny dressed and ready for whatever. He found my coffee maker and made a pot already!

"Hope I made it to your liking, John," Benny said.

"Hell, Benny," I replied. "Don't you know an "Alky" will drink almost anything, even coffee."

I went and found my cup and filled it.

"Well Benny, today is the big day, when you tell your story to your fellows," I told him.

"I know, John," Benny replied. "For some reason, I'm not all that worried about doing that."

"Good," John replied. "Just speak from the heart and God will take care of the rest."

Marie came out of the spare bedroom and asked, "Did you two save me any of that coffee I smell?"

"Yep," I replied. "And if you like it, it was Benny who made it this morning."

"I've drank his coffee before and it didn't kill me, so let me at it," Marie laughed.

While we were sitting around my kitchen table drinking our morning coffee, Marie said, "John, I want to thank you for helping Benny to get better and for all you have done for him."

"Marie," I said. "It's what we do for one another. I helped him and let me tell you, tonight he is going to help a hell of a lot of alcoholics."

I looked at Benny. Then, gave him a big thumbs up and he gave me back a grin. That made me smile. Marie asked to use the shower. I told her fresh washcloths, soap and towels were in there waiting for her. Later, we went to Kristina's restaurant for breakfast. After that, I asked if they would like to see the giant redwoods up close. They both said 'yes'.

We loaded up in my car and headed south. When I got to Pepperwood, I pulled off the main road and went to the lower road, which was The Avenue of The Giants road. I pulled off where not too long ago, where I had found the money. I did the same and parked.

"John, is this the place?" Benny asked me. Then, said no more.

Marie did not know what we were talking about. She opened her door, got out of the car and stared at the giant trees that reached for the sky.

"My God, John," Marie said to me, "If I wasn't seeing this with my own eyes, I would not believe what I am looking at."

Benny said," I think he got his point across when, John said big and tall."

As we strolled through Benny said, "I wonder if Robin Hood ever passed through these parts, John."

I got his meaning and laughed and said, "I don't know, but I'm sure that he'd like it here."

"What the hell are you talking about?" Marie asked.

Benny chuckled and said, "We're just being silly and if you want to, you can join us."

It was time to go back to Eureka and get ready for tonight's speaker meeting.

The Speakers Meeting

It was seven O'clock and a half hour, before Benny was going to speak. I was checking to see if everything was in order. One thing about A.A., you can always get help if you ask for it.

But, you gotta ask. I was the 10-minute speaker that night that went before Benny as the lead speaker. I asked if it was OK if I announced

Benny when it was time for him to speak. They said that it would be fine.

I did my talk on service and how important I believed it was for all of us. Then, I got the nod. I went to the stage and behind the podium.

"Ladies and gentlemen," I said. "You all know me, at least most of you do. I want to introduce you to a man I picked up on the road hiking his way home. Since then, we have become real close friends. So, let me introduce Benny L. from Gallup New Mexico."

"Hello, I'm Benny Luna; Navajo Indian from the high country of Gallup New Mexico," Benny said. "I'm going to tell you who and what I am, what I am, what happened to me and tell you what it is like now."

He told them of his childhood, how he felt like he never fit in the Indian or the white man world. Benny was speaking from his heart and the people were listening with theirs.

I stopped looking at him and started looking at the people in the crowd in front of him. They were feeling his words. He told them about Mitch and how he pulled him out of an alley in Barstow and offered him some stew that he did not want.

About how Mitch held his head when he was puking up his guts, how he stayed up all night weening him off the wine he was on.

Then, he started talking about recovery, about how he wanted to live again and get back in his family, even if it took the rest of his life. So, when he looked at Marie, she knew he meant it. When he was winding up his talk, there was a man in a chair up front to the left side of the stage and if one looked closely, you would see tears on his cheeks.

BAM, Benny and John Meet

Benny ended his talk to a standing ovation. He then stepped down from the stage and the people swarmed him, shaking his hand, slapping him on the back, waving at him and whatever else they could do to get his attention. After a while, it let up and the man in the front chair walked up to Benny and asked him if he could have a few words with him and me.

Benny flagged me over to the man. I knew that he wanted to speak to both of us. I walked over and he introduced himself to us.

"My name is Bam. Benny, your share tonight brought me to my knees. John, I've been following you for quite some time now. "

"You're one tough critter to find with all your travels. I am the one that tossed that bag of money down the hill that you found."

I was scared and my arms hairs stood up. Is he going to kill me? Is he going to turn me into the cops? My mind was racing and all I could do was wait to see what was next. Benny too was amazed and stood his ground for me to feel safe.

"I've been in Eureka for some time and hanging out at The Club in the morning and going to meetings," Bam told us. "I found out all about you John and the good things that you have done to turn people's lives around by using that money I stole. Don't worry. That money was a curse and lead me into doing things I will have to live with for the rest of my life. My higher power told me to let you keep the money and start a new life like you and Benny."

Benny and I were in utter amazement! You could tell that this large man could have waited outside to get the money and beaten me to death.

I had no idea what to say. I just stood there waiting to see what was next.

"While I was here and started to sober up, I made a few calls and got hired to work for a security company setting up and fixing alarms that I used to disarm to steal money from people's houses," Bam told us. "I'm heading out of town right now and wanted to make sure you are safe and clear with me. God bless you, John. Believe it or not, you saved my life."

Someone started blinking the lights to let us know that it was time to start leaving the place. Bam left and the rest of us started wrapping things up.

Benny said, "God must love you a lot, John. Now, please take Marie and I to your home."

Epilogue

One Year Later

BAM

Let's start where we had ended with, Bam Davis, the night he went to the speakers meeting in Eureka to get his money back or so he thought. When The little Indian got up and spoke to the people of which he is one of.

The little fella was talking to Bam when he wanted to change his life. He was tired of being empty inside. He seen a man who had what he wanted and was willing to go to any length to get it.

Right then and there he said to himself, "to hell with the goddamn money! I'm not going to hurt people anymore and I'm tired of running and going to prison for my actions." So, he went back to the little room that he had rented and started on his new way of life. He didn't know how he was going to do it, but if that little Indian did it then, so can I. The money sack was still in the Bronco; 150 grand. I hope God thinks it's alright to keep it because, it will sure help me start my new life.

He got to thinking one evening about all the places he had broken into and thought about the alarm systems he has passed. He thought, "I wonder if they might hire a guy who used to cause them trouble. Maybe, give me a job." So, what the hell, he wrote them a letter and damn if they didn't write him back and offered him an interview which he took them up on.

To shorten this, they found out that Bam had a hell of a brain and they hired him! He told them that he wanted to work out of his home. When they came up with a new system, they would send him one and he would try to break it down. He thought to himself, "Here I am getting paid for what I used to go to prison for! Crazy world, huh?"

He remembered the name of the little town in Oregon and he wanted to see if he could find his mother. When his health got better, he went there and found a cousin who helped him find her. She was working in a little cafe and seemed to be doing alright. She started crying as soon as she found out who he was. He held her hand and told her that it was alright and that he loved her and that he understood why she left.

He told her he had led a rocky and rough life, but that he was starting over and wanted to know if they could start their lives over together. He got her phone number and mailing address and told her he would keep in touch with her.

"Oh yeah, Mom, I never forgot what you told me when I was a little boy and that is, 'good people live in Oregon.'"

Benny and Marie Luna

Spending the last days of their trip to California and the wonderful redwoods, they told John that they would like to return and do this again. John drove them down to San Francisco where they caught a plane back to Albuquerque. Before they left Eureka, John said he had something to do in town that he would be right back and did.

Then, went into his bedroom and closed the door. He was soon back out and handed Benny a briefcase and said he wanted him to have it and take it home with them. He said that they would open it when they got to Marie's house. Benny smiled then; told John he would do just that.

After Stubby picked Marie and Benny up a the airport and dropped them off at Marie's place, they went in, kicked off their shoes, found a chair and started to relax. Benny opened it and they dumped the wrapped bills on her table long with a note John had put in with the money. Benny grabbed the note, then read it to **Marie.**

"There is 30 thousand here. It is for your son's college education. I hope it will help him get started in life. Spend it anyway you want to. Please, come back to see me as soon as you can. The time you spent here in Eureka with me, I will carry forever. Until then, Love John."

They looked at each other, then Marie started crying. Benny went over to her and put his arms around her and held her a long, long time.

"Our son will be able to go to college; if he wants to." Benny told Marie.

So, it began. Benny bought a table to set up in the back yard with the owner's permission. It was big, round one with a pole in the middle with an umbrella on top. Then, they bought some lawn chairs to go around it.

Every weekend, he would spend at least one day visiting Marie in the back yard when, the weather was good. Slowly, ever so slowly, Danny's attitude towards Benny began to change for the better. Benny didn't push, he let go and let God do what he could not do himself. The world didn't know it yet, but one of the best mile runners in the world would soon be showing himself.

Kathy and Little Alice

Kathy was still working at Mission Linen, but she recently got a raise and a better position where she is working. Sometimes she thinks about what happened in her and Alice's life in the last few months and it is pretty hard to believe. Out of nowhere, a man up and gives her a new car, 2005 Dodge Caravan.

It was not brand new, but it was new to her. Compared to what she had before, it was the best in the world! Out of nowhere he gives her money to help her dig herself out of a hole.

That man called not long ago to find out how Alice was doing. She was happy to tell him that their lives were on the upswing. She had a new boyfriend in her life, but she was not going to leap into a new relationship until, she found out where it was leading to. She was not going to go down "Heartache Hill" again.

Now, for Little Alice. A thousand words would not be able to explain what was inside that small body of hers. All the brightness, wonder, love and goodness that she gives to those around her. Growing like a weed, this little 5 and ½ year old is ready to show her soon to be classmates what first grade is all about.

John Stone

The first thing John Stone, Robin Hood of The Redwoods would want to tell you is that he is not a hero or anything close to being one. He is a simple man who found a backpack full of money and wanted to help some of the people he met in his travels.

He would like you to think of him as a good man. One who tells people from time to time, to do the best you can with what you got and leave the rest up to God. John will keep on doing what has kept him going all these years since, he has stopped drinking. He has decided to try and give back what has been freely given to him. So, who knows, maybe somewhere down the road yours and his paths may cross. If that happens, I hope you shake his hand and wish the old gray beard well.

So, I will close with these words. John says to all his close friends, "Remember, God loves you and so does old John Stone."

About the Author

Thomas "Tom" Lewis was the 12th child born into a family of 13 siblings. His parents came west in 1937 from Oklahoma to California and worked in the fields picking cotton, cutting grapes and fruit. Seeing his share of hard times, Tom grew up early and decided to join the Army at 17.

At the age of 20, he got himself into the logging industry. He then began to work on the highways in Northern California doing labor.

Having had a stroke and a heart attack in 1999, everything seemed to come to a complete stop. He went into a deep depression. That is when Connie Cook came into his life. Tom told her that he wanted to write a book. With support of her and help of many friends, he did so.

Ever the dreamer, Tom had visions of man finding a back pack full of money and what he would do with it.

"I hope that you enjoy reading this story" Thomas *"Tom" Lewis*

Made in the USA
Middletown, DE
27 September 2020